P9-AOH-174

The lovely young lady was a witch and a traveler.

That's right. She's me.

The
Ashen Witch
ELAINA

A young genius
who earned the title of
"witch," the highest rank
for a mage, at the tender
age of fifteen.

©Azure

"I'll never forget you!"

The
Stardust
Witch
FRAN
Elaina's
teacher.

"As you
travel, my
students and
I will be
cheering you
on with all
our hearts.
Never forget
that."

WANDERING WITCH
The Journey of Elaina
CONTENTS

◆ • ◆

WANDERING WITCH
The Journey of Elaina

JOUGI SHIRAISHI

Illustration
AZURE

1

YEN ON

NEW YORK

WANDERING WITCH
The Journey of Elaina

JOUGI SHIRAISHI

Translation by Nicole Wilder
Cover art by Azure

MAJO NO TABITABI vol. 1
Copyright © 2016 Jougi Shiraishi
Illustrations copyright © 2016 Azure
All rights reserved.
Original Japanese edition published in 2016 by SB Creative Corp.
This English edition is published by arrangement with SB Creative Corp., Tokyo, in care of Tuttle-Mori Agency, Inc., Tokyo.

English translation © 2020 by Yen Press, LLC

Yen On
150 West 30th Street, 19th Floor
New York, NY 10001

Visit us at yenpress.com ✷ facebook.com/yenpress ✷ twitter.com/yenpress ✷ yenpress.tumblr.com ✷ instagram.com/yenpress

First Yen On Edition: January 2020

Yen On is an imprint of Yen Press, LLC.
The Yen On name and logo are trademarks of Yen Press, LLC.

The publisher is not responsible for websites (or their content) that are not owned by the publisher.

Library of Congress Cataloging-in-Publication Data
Names: Shiraishi, Jougi, author. | Azure, illustrator. | Wilder, Nicole, translator.
Title: Wandering Witch : the journey of Elaina / Jougi Shiraishi ; illustration by Azure ; translation by Nicole Wilder.
Other titles: Majo no tabitabi. English
Description: First Yen On edition. | New York, NY : Yen On, 2020–
Identifiers: LCCN 2019052222 | ISBN 9781975332952 (volume 1 ; trade paperback)
Subjects: CYAC: Fantasy. | Witches—Fiction. | Voyages and travels—Fiction.
Classification: LCC PZ7.1.S517725 Wan 2020 | DDC [Fic]—dc23
LC record available at https://lccn.loc.gov/2019052222

ISBNs: 978-1-9753-3295-2 (paperback)
        978-1-9753-3311-9 (ebook)

10 9 8 7 6 5 4 3 2

LSC-C

Printed in the United States of America

WANDERING WITCH
The Journey of Elaina

CHAPTER 1

The Country of Mages

It was a quiet country, surrounded by rugged, forbidding mountains and hidden behind tall walls. Nobody from the outside world could visit.

Above a rock face shimmering with heat in the brilliant sunlight, a single broom soared through the warm air. The one guiding it on its way was a beautiful young girl. She wore a black robe and a pointy hat, and her ashen hair flapped in the wind. If anyone had been around to notice her, they would have turned to look, wondering with a sigh who that beauty on the broom could be...

That's right. She's me.

Ah, that was a joke.

"...Almost there."

The high wall looked like it had been carved out of the mountain itself. Glancing downward just a bit, I spotted the gate and steered my broom toward it.

It had taken some serious work to get to this country, but I suppose the people who lived here had planned it that way—to keep people from entering by mistake. After all, there's no way anyone would trek all the way out here without a very good reason.

I dismounted my broom just in front of the gate. A local sentry, apparently conducting immigration inspections, stepped up to meet me.

After looking me over slowly from head to toe and examining the brooch on my chest, he smiled cheerfully.

"Welcome to the Country of Mages. Right this way, Madam Witch."

"Hmm? Don't you need to test whether I can do magic or not?"

I had heard that anyone visiting this country had to prove their magical ability to enter; anyone who didn't meet a certain standard would be turned away.

"I saw you fly in. And besides, that brooch you're wearing means you're a witch. So please, go on ahead."

Oh yeah, that's right. Being able to fly on a broom is one of the minimum prerequisites for entry. Of course they could see my approach from the gatehouse. How silly of me!

After bowing slightly to the guard, I passed through the massive gate. Here was the mages' country. Novice magic users, apprentices, and full-fledged witches—as long as you could use magic, you were permitted into this curious country, while everyone else was turned away.

As I passed through the huge gate, two strange signboards standing side by side caught my eye. I peered at them in confusion.

The first sign depicted a mage straddling a broom, enclosed in a circle. The sign beside it showed the image of a soldier walking, surrounded by a triangle.

What's with these signs?

I knew the answer as soon as I looked up—above the crowded brickwork houses and beneath the gleaming sun, mages of all kinds were streaking across the sky in every direction.

I see. It must be a rule in countries where they only permit mages to enter—most everyone's flying around on a broom, so very few people choose to walk.

Satisfied with my explanation for the signboards, I pulled out my broom and sat on it sideways. With a push off the ground, I gently floated up into the air in a living demonstration of the signboard.

"So flying is the preferred mode of transportation here, huh?"

And with that, I saw the mages' country as it was meant to be seen. Above the reddish-brown roofs stretched out like so much dry earth, mages drifted through the air. Some had stopped their brooms to have a friendly chat, while others flew by with bundles of baggage tied to their brooms. There were suspicious, witchy-looking old women as well as children racing through the sky, vying to see who could fly higher.

These people must live their whole lives in the air.

It was a really wonderful scene. It almost took my breath away.

I joined their ranks, soaring above the country, aimlessly surrendering to the flow of air traffic around me. Suddenly a sign secured to the top of one of the roofs caught my eye. It was apparently an INN. I passed it without stopping and saw the word GROCER next. There were others: a BUTCHER and even a JEWELER. As I suspected, life here was lived above the rooftops, and placing your signs on top of the roof must have been common practice.

Looking around, I saw that the roofs on most houses had a window built in that was large enough for a single person to pass through. As I watched absently, one of those windows opened, and a man riding a broom flew out.

So that's *what they're used for.*

I flew around at a leisurely pace, slowly taking in the scenery, until—

"Ahhhhhhhhhhhhhhh!"

—a scream came from behind me. Steadying my broom with one hand, I held on to my hat so it wouldn't fly away and turned around.

Ah, too late.

"Ahhhhhhhhhhh!"

Careening directly toward me at a preposterous speed, like a screaming meteorite trailing a tail of tears, the person in question was already only about one rooftop away by the time I spotted them.

Dodge? Impossible.

I reflexively turned my upper body away, but there was no avoiding the collision. With a series of grunts ("Ugya!" "Geh"), we tangled together and crashed into the rooftop below. The neatly lined tiles sheared off with a clatter and crunch, and we finally came to a halt just shy of falling off the edge of the roof. I saw a single tile bounce off the ground far below. Thank goodness there weren't any pedestrians.

The angle had been shallow, and I had avoided a direct collision with the ground. Plus, the strange person who had collided with me had taken the brunt of the landing, so thankfully I was uninjured.

I clambered to my feet, brushing at a few reddish-brown shards of roofing that were stuck to my black robe.

"……"

"Urggggh…"

The teenage girl groaning and looking around in a daze appeared to be just a little bit younger than me. Her black hair was cut short and even all the way around, and she had an androgynous-looking face. She wore a white blouse and a checkered skirt under a black mantle, both of which were in serious disarray after she got caught underneath me.

She isn't wearing a brooch or anything on her chest, so she must be a novice.

"…Um, are you all right?"

When I touched the fallen girl's shoulder, she opened her eyes.

"……"

"……" She was silent.

It seemed like she was still struggling to process the situation, so I ventured, "Do you have trouble steering your broom?"

Yes, I'll admit I was being a touch sarcastic.

"…Ah."

"Looks like you've finally come your senses," I said with a smile.

"Ahhhh!" She looked around again. "Wh-wh-wh-what do I do? What do I do? There's no way I can fix this many tiles…"

Hey, now… "How about an apology first?"

"Ah, s-sorry! It wasn't on purpose! Really!"

Well, I knew that. "Anyway, are you all right? You flew in like a hurricane."

"Oh, I'm fine! I'm in tip-top shape, see?!" the girl said, as small rivulets of red ran down from her head. Her eyes were clear, and she had no trouble speaking.

......

"You're bleeding. From your head."

"That's just sweat!"

"Does your sweat always smell like iron?"

"Um, well, um… It's sweat!"

"Okay, I get it, so just calm down a little."

"Yes, ma'am!"

"......"

I'm not sure why, but I already feel exhausted. Maybe it's from the collision.

I had been planning to make the girl fix the broken tiles after a good scolding, but enough was enough. She was already a mess; forcing her to repair the roof when she was in this state would just be heartless. Instead, I took my handkerchief out of my pocket.

"Here, have this. Press it to your head."

"Oh…but…"

"Also, I'm going to put the roof tiles back now, so go take a rest over there, please."

"No, I'll help, too!"

"In your condition, if you tried to help, you'd just be in the way. Go rest," I told her in no uncertain terms.

"But—"

"You're. In. My. Way."

"…Okay."

Like a stray cat, the dejected young girl sat down on the peak of the roof and pressed the handkerchief against her head wound. As energetic as she had seemed, it was clear she had pushed herself a little too hard. The very moment she sat down, she slouched over and collapsed.

I can put off dealing with her for a bit. It's not like she's going to die from her injury or anything. First, let's do something about this disaster here…

I gathered magical energy in my hands. Instantly, a long, thin wand appeared in my grasp, accompanied by a faint glow.

This was the special privilege of mages. We're able to produce anything—wands and brooms and other magical tools, for example—out of thin air.

I channeled energy into my wand and set to work.

It was a time-reversing spell.

As the name might suggest, it's a type of magic that fixes broken things and heals injuries by making time run in reverse. It requires slightly advanced magical ability, but any witch living in this country should have been able to perform it. I'm sure it would have been difficult for the little novice out cold behind me, though.

The roof tiles began to move as I showered them with magic. The broken tiles stuck themselves back together, returning to their original places like so many puzzle pieces.

After all the fragments had vanished and any sign of an accident had been wiped away, I completed the spell and turned around. Now it was time to fix up the girl.

"Okay, you're next."

"Um, uhhh…"

I approached the girl, who sat up nervously holding her head, and applied the spell. Beneath the gentle light, her tattered clothes mended themselves and her injuries healed instantly.

"Whoa…" I could hear her mumble.

It's nothing impressive, though. Once you become a witch, this stuff is a cinch.

After making sure that she was in good shape, I hurried over to pick up the brooms that had fallen onto the roof. I decided it was probably a good idea to get out of there before making any more of a scene.

"Oh, um!"

The girl apparently had more to say to me, but I threw one leg over my broom, halfway ignoring her. "You don't need to apologize. Just don't forget to look where you're going when you're flying around on your broom, okay?"

"Please wait, I have to do something to make up for—"

"No need. I'm in a hurry. Good-bye, nameless novice."

And so I got back on my broom and flew away.

○

Any human who can use magic starts their training as a novice. Not everyone can become one, and in most cases the ability is passed down through blood. My parents were novices, too.

Apprentice witches rank above novices, but they're one level below full witches. As the name suggests, the title of "witch" applies only to girls and women. I have no idea why, but women naturally have greater magical ability than men. That's why only women can attain ranks higher than novice.

There's only one way to become an apprentice: pass the magic exams and receive the corsage that proves your status. There is no alternative method. However, the exams are brutal, and many people drop out before they reach the end.

After becoming an apprentice witch, one undergoes a very specific training regimen to earn the title of "witch." This means long days of hard work under the watchful eye of a proper witch, until the apprentice finally wins her approval. The training might last a single day, or it might take ten years. It all depends on the individual's own efforts and on the witch who is serving as her teacher.

When someone is officially recognized as a witch, she receives a star-shaped brooch with her name engraved on the back, and her teacher gives her a witch title. Mine is "the Ashen Witch."

That was a pretty long-winded explanation, but my point is that as a full-fledged witch, I should have ranked among the top magic users in this country. I had expected that people would look up at me with envy as I flew through the sky, that when I went to a restaurant they would tell me, "Madam Witch! Allow me to offer you a discount on everything on the menu! Please, eat to your heart's content!" and so on, but…

"Huh? A discount? We don't do anything like that. Are you saying you don't have any money, missy?"

"……"

So that's how it is, hmm? I suppose if the restaurant gave special treatment to each and every witch, they'd go out of business.

I left the restaurant and went to the jeweler's next. I wanted to sell a jewel that I had picked up in one of the countries I had visited before this one, and I was expecting a considerable sum from it.

"Ah, this here's a total counterfeit, see? I can't give you anything for it."

"Surely there's been a mistake. Take a closer look, please."

"I can look all ya want, but the answer's gonna be the same. Whaddaya wanna do? If you don't need it, I can get rid of it for you…"

"…That just sounds like you're scheming to steal it from me, doesn't it?"

"Of course not, sweetie! I'd never do that to ya. So what'll it be?"

"Give it back."

By the time I left the jeweler's, I was in a sour mood.

Well, I'm sure the owner of that jewelry shop is just a bit of a swindler, that's all. It's not like he was treating me specifically with contempt, right? …Right?

Feeling uneasy, I headed for an inn. The day was drawing to a close. However—

"Hey. This isn't a place for kids like you. Go on, scram."

…Huuuh? What on earth? Is this some kind of upper-crust hotel exclusively for rich people? Hmm… Either way, I'm not staying here. Let's go somewhere else.

I hopped off my broom atop a very cheap-looking inn with a tattered sign. *Surely this place won't turn me away.*

I opened the window on the roof and descended the ladder that led inside. But halfway down I couldn't be bothered anymore, so I jumped.

Thud. The sound echoed through the building like a cannonball.

Hey, I'm not that heavy. Rude.

I had dropped into the reception area.

The girl seated behind the counter looked at me. "Welco—"

She stiffened.

So did I.

She had short black hair. Boyish, androgynous features.

Sitting there in front of me was the girl who had (literally) run into me several hours earlier.

"......"

"......"

She was the first to shake herself loose from the frozen moment in time.

"E-eeeeeek! I'm s-s-sorry! I'm sorry! Are you here for revenge? This is revenge, isn't it?! I'm sorry! Spare my life! Spare meee!"

"No, uh..."

"Waaaaaah! I don't wanna diiiiiiiie!"

"Um..." *No need for hysterics; come on.*

She was grinding her head against the counter and sobbing. "Just spare my liiife..."

I touched her shoulder lightly.

"Eek! You're going to tear me limb from limb? Are you going for my shoulder first? Noooooo!"

Could you please be quiet for one second? —Wait, no, don't say that aloud. "Um, it's all right? I just came to stay at this inn tonight."

"Nooooo— Oh, is that all? In that case, please fill out this form."

"......"

There were several things I would have liked to say, but I refrained. Setting her off again would be more than I could handle right now.

I took the form from her and picked up a quill pen from its stand on the counter. It was a simple piece of paperwork, just asking the number of people and number of nights, plus the name of a representative. As an experienced traveler, I had quickly grown accustomed to these kinds of forms.

As I moved the quill pen smoothly across the paper, the girl spoke up in a very bright voice. "I'm really sorry for what happened this afternoon. Whenever my mind wanders during practice, I seem to lose the ability to steer the broom…"

"I see." *In other words, you're a bad flier.*

"I really wanted to thank you properly, but you sped off— Ah, so your name is Elaina. I'm Saya." She smiled cheerfully at me as she watched me write.

"You don't really need to thank me," I replied as I continued filling out the form. "Besides, plenty of people get tangled up with others when practicing magic."

Come to think of it, I once set my house on fire trying to light a candle. My parents really chewed me out for that one. Oh, to be young again…

"But won't you let me do something for you? I caused all that trouble for you, and you even healed my injuries. I'd hate to leave things as they are."

"It's really fine, but…"

"Anything is okay! Please! Miss Elaina!"

I shook my head as the girl begged me to let her pay me back. I'm sure it would have been strange to watch.

Well, it's not as if she's asking me to go out of my way for her, so there's no need to dig in my heels. I gave it a little thought as I was writing.

"Hmm…well then, in that case—" *How about I get you to give me a discount on the room?* I was about to ask, then stopped myself.

An item on the form had caught my eye. SPECIAL DISCOUNT FOR WITCHES (HALF-OFF ONE NIGHT) it read.

Oh-ho! What have we here?

"Ah, that discount doesn't apply to anyone who's not a witch. Ordinary mages should circle the regular price option," she said, knitting her eyebrows.

"I see." I circled SPECIAL DISCOUNT FOR WITCHES (HALF-OFF ONE NIGHT).

"Eh? No, um… Huh?"

What's with that weird reaction? Sheesh, rude. "I *am* a witch, so…"

"Come on, you can't joke about that… Oh, well, but I did cause you a bunch of trouble… Okay! I'll go ahead and apply the discount!" She clapped her hands once.

I had a feeling that we were somehow talking past each other, which was making me nervous. I shook my head. "No, no, no, that's not it. You see, I *am* a witch. Can't you see how I'm dressed?"

"Huh?" she said, pointing at my chest. "But you don't have a witch's brooch."

"I beg your pardon?"

Following her finger, I lowered my eyes to my own chest.

The brooch that belonged there had disappeared.

○

In a sense, a witch's brooch is her identification. Without it, I was just a traveler who could use magic.

That must be why the last inn treated me like a little child. I see, I see. But how did I only just notice that it was missing? Witches aren't all that rare, and if I had been just a little more skeptical, I could have done something earlier. Am I just an idiot? Ugh, screw you, Elaina!

As I cursed and swore at myself, I searched frantically for the brooch.

"…It's gone."

It was nowhere to be found.

I must have dropped it when Saya and I collided, but it was already completely dark outside. The brooch was small enough to fit in the palm of my hand…not exactly the kind of thing I could find just by groping around in the dark.

"…Ugh."

After scouring the roof in a thorough zigzag pattern and looking into all the cracks between tiles, I went down to ground level and searched all around the house. But of course, no luck.

I'm gonna cry.

"I didn't find anything!! Miss Elaina, it's not over here, either!!" An obnoxiously loud voice came from the rooftop, echoing down the alleyway. When I looked up, I saw Saya illuminated by the moonlight.

Right after we had discovered the brooch was missing, she had said, "This is my fault, too, so I'm going with you!" and insisted on joining me in my search. She had left another person in charge at the inn or something, I guess.

While I was walking around below, I had let her take the roof on the off chance that I had overlooked something. But apparently, she hadn't fared any better.

I floated up beside her on my broom.

"We've done a thorough search and the brooch isn't here. We have to consider the possibility that someone picked it up..." I let out a deep sigh.

"I think it's also going to be hard to find because it's dark outside," Saya said. "It might be good to search here again tomorrow morning." Her voice was cheerful, though my shoulders were slumped with disappointment. I was a little grateful for her optimism.

"I'll do that..." I nodded meekly at her suggestion and turned to head back to the inn.

Flying around unsteadily on my broom, I must have looked just like a mere apprentice witch who was still learning how to steer. *Ah, if anyone were to fly close to me, I just might collide with them.*

I had gone through a lot to get that brooch, and it held a lot of memories of my time with my teacher. Losing it was a bitter pill to swallow.

If I had lost it when I first became a witch, I'm sure I would have noticed right away. But after wearing it every day for two years, I was probably too accustomed to just always having it on me.

"*…Sigh.*"

This was depressing.

After the search, I returned to the inn and ate dinner, then entered my room using the key I got from Saya, remembered I hadn't taken a bath yet, and headed straight for the big bathroom instead.

I soaked in the hot water for a whole hour as my mind wandered. *Ah, I must have dropped it when I collided with Saya…but it wasn't there… How mysterious…* I stretched out almost fully and filled the big bathtub (I was alone). Then, just before I melted away into the hot water, I sat my heavy body back up.

And then I went back to my room…

"Ah, hello—"

…and found Saya inside.

I closed the door. I took a step back and checked the room number. *Yep, it matches the number written on the key. Strange. Maybe I was just seeing things?*

I opened the door once again.

"Ah, hello—"

If only it had been a bad dream… But alas, there was no mistaking it: Saya was in my room, giving me a carefree wave from atop the hard bed.

……

"…What are you doing in my room?" I closed the door with a hand behind my back.

"I wanted to talk to you, Elaina, so I waited here for you."

"I thought I locked the door."

"You sure did! But I work here!" She proudly pulled out a key ring with a large number of keys.

I walked up to her without a word and grabbed both of her cheeks.

"Ow, dhad hurtsh! Id hurtsh!"

"What's the big idea, entering a person's room without permission? Huh?" I pulled hard on her cheeks.

"*Dhey're gonna teahw! You'we teahwing bwy cheeks!*" *They're gonna tear, you're tearing my cheeks* is what she seemed to want to say.

"Hmm? What's that? I can't hear you."

"Waaaaaah…"

I pulled and twisted her tender cheeks until I was satisfied and released her.

Massaging her slightly red cheeks with both hands, Saya muttered, "That was mean…" Really, though, which one of us was actually in the wrong here?

"Well, what did you want? You made a point of waiting in my room, so you must have some reason for it, right?"

Still massaging her face, Saya said, "Miss Elaina, you're really a witch, right?"

"Yeah, well," I confirmed, "I don't have my brooch at the moment, but yes, I'm a witch."

"Then that means you passed the magic exam, right?"

"I did."

Even now I remembered how disappointed I was by the lack of challenge.

Saya stared at me for a moment, then suddenly got down off the bed and knelt down. Then she placed both hands on the floor and pressed her forehead to the ground.

"Please help me! Teach me the secrets to passing the exam, please!"

"…Um, what are you doing on the floor like that?"

"This is the traditional way of prostrating ourselves in my hometown! It's a surefire technique used when you've done something unforgivable to the other party."

What a strange tradition… Do the people in her hometown have to apologize to others that often? Still, you can really feel the sincerity.

But it gave me this…what's the word? Weird feeling? Creepy, even?

Repressing the urge to say, "*Huuuh? You think that's all it takes to ask a favor like that?*" I knelt down beside her.

"Um, just take your head off the floor for now."

"You'll do it?!" She stared up at me.

"Take it easy," I said. "First, tell me about your situation."

She told me.

I let her sit on the bed again, and I pulled out the cheap-looking chair from the desk and sat facing her. Saya gave her black hair a slight shake and tilted her head, then hesitantly opened her mouth.

"Um... So I have a younger sister. She's very cute."

"Okay..." *That's a pretty weird way to start, but I've already committed.*

"We come from a country far to the east. My sister and I came all this way to become apprentice witches—there are no organizations offering the exams in our hometown. So the two of us worked at this inn and saved money while studying for the exams. We lived that way for several years, but..."

"But the two of you are still just novices?"

She cast her eyes downward and shook her head slowly. "Only my sister took the latest round of exams. And she went home. Without me."

"...Hmm." *I see, I see. I think I know where this is going. In other words...*

"Your cute little sister has surpassed you, and you got so impatient that you decided to rope a witch you just met—in an accident, might I add—into helping you pass your exams? Is that it?"

Scratching her cheek in apparent embarrassment, Saya mumbled, "Well, um...that's...yeah, more or less."

"So when is the next exam?"

"One week from now... I don't have much time..."

You've taken the advancement exams several times, so I don't think there's any need to panic. But you're probably so worried about it because you want to see your sister again.

"......"

Breaking the silence, I spoke. "I'll help you for as long as it takes me to find my brooch." I couldn't leave the country until I had found my brooch anyway, and I wouldn't have anything to do when I wasn't searching. She would probably even let me stay at the inn for free, so I thought it sounded like a good idea.

O

In order to be promoted to the level of apprentice witch, you have to pass a written exam and then a practical magical skills exam.

The written exam is simple, and so long as you can drill magic theory, history, and other subjects into your head, nothing could be easier, really. But then there's the practical exam. There's no way around it; without real ability, you'll have to take it over and over again.

As for the contents of the practical exam, they mainly look at two skills: your ability to fly a broom and how you handle offensive magic. Each time the exam is given, only one person may pass. The exam being given in one week's time would be no different. Winding through the sky on a broom, each aspiring witch would attack the others, trying to take down her opponents while protecting herself. The last one left would pass the exam and be declared an apprentice witch publicly.

The battles were always violent and hard to watch. The nastiest parts of human nature always seemed to be on full display. I would never want to take the exam again.

"I've got to tell you honestly, Saya. With the ability you possess right now, no matter how earnestly you fight, the chance that you can win against the other candidates is pretty close to zero," I said from atop my broom. It was early in the morning the day after I had promised to help her. "However, close to zero doesn't mean absolute zero. Set your mind at ease."

"Wh-what should I do?!" She was energetic even in the early morning, and her eyes sparkled with excitement. She was as radiant as the morning sun.

I steered my broom over to where she was sitting on the tiled roof, knees folded under her. "First, I'll teach you to control your broom at least as well as I can, if not better."

"Aw… That seems a little tough…" She wrinkled her nose.

Tough? I'm going easy on you.

"There's no other way to keep up during the practical skills exam. If you go in at your current skill level, you'll probably fall off the moment the exam starts and waste another chance. You've got to avoid that at least."

"Rgh…"

So that's where we're at.

First, I set her to work improving this most basic of magical skills. Just as I had imagined, Saya could barely even fly. (It was so bad that I was ready to question whether I should even call her a mage at all!) I really had to put her through the wringer.

Ah, so this is what mothers feel like teaching their children how to fly on brooms…

We trained from morning until night, as long as the day would allow. We persevered with our crash course even when the neighborhood children flying freely around us started sneering and pointing.

Naturally, I had not forgotten about searching for my brooch. Saya had seen gradual improvement, but I hadn't made any progress at all.

Seriously, where in the world is my brooch?

"Next is turning. Smoothly shift your body weight and make a quick turn, please."

"Okay!"

"Next is emergency braking and speed boosts. Use the full weight of your body and pull the broom hard to stop it, then burst forward like you're kicking the sky."

"Okay!"

"Next is midair dismounts. After letting go of the broom midair, use magic to call it back. I'll help you out if you get into trouble, so don't worry and just fly."

"Okay!"

"Next is—" Okay, you get the idea.

In the end, Saya quickly learned to control her broom almost as well as I could. As for how many days it took for her to reach that level? Only two! I had coaxed some amazing improvements out of her. *Really makes you wonder what she's been doing before now…or perhaps it's my teaching that's so good?*

When I asked her, Saya told me bashfully, "Until now, I've only studied by myself."

Well, there's your problem.

It was the fourth day of my stay in this country—and the third day of our intensive training regimen. Unlike the search for my brooch, which had not seen any headway (though I had simply been asking around), Saya's education was progressing rapidly and didn't seem like it would stop anytime soon.

"Next, let's study some offensive spells—how is your wind magic?"

"Wind magic?" Saya sat atop the scorched reddish-brown roof, head tilted.

I nodded once and answered, "Yes, wind. By controlling the flow of the air, you can block the other participants."

This was the slightly unconventional method that I had used during my own practical exam. Changing the flow of the air had been surprisingly effective, and even now I remembered how the other contestants had lost their balance and fallen from their brooms or swerved into buildings.

Wind control was both easy to learn and a powerful weapon. If we had enough time, I definitely wanted to teach her.

"Well then, hit that can over there with a blast of wind, please."

I pointed at the cans we had set up on the peak of the roof across from us. There was about one house's worth of distance between us and the cans, so it wasn't a difficult task at all.

"It works best if you visualize making a ball of air and hitting the cans with it—like so."

I waved my wand, and instantly, a strong wind grazed one of the cans. It teetered back and forth with a clatter.

I turned to face Saya, who was looking at me dubiously. *"It didn't fall down, did it? Did you mess up?"* she seemed to be asking.

But I did that on purpose. Really!

"All right, give it a try."

"...L-like this?"

With a *whoosh*, Saya waved her wand. Air magic is one of the first types of magic a novice witch learns, so she was able to produce a gust of wind, but it merely rushed over the tops of the cans. *Too bad.*

"You're holding the wand wrong. You're pointing it wrong, too. Wind magic is subtle, so trying to force it won't help."

"Um, okay, how about this?"

Whoosh. The wind flew right past the can, exactly as before.

"Wrong. Like this."

I waved my wand, and the cans clattered against each other again. Saya let out a small noise of surprise. "Whoa..." She had finally realized I was trying *not* to knock the cans down.

And then she waved her wand again, more gently this time, with a little "Ey!" She had clearly learned from watching me, but the force behind her magic was too weak. It only produced a light breeze.

...This isn't going well.

"Not quite. Like this."

"Like this?"

Swing and a miss.

"Totally wrong. Like this."

"H-how's this?!"

The wind didn't even brush the cans.

"Just awful. Like this, watch."

"Something like this, then!"

......

It was a lost cause. Truly. My instructions made no difference whatsoever.

Time to kick things up a notch. I went around behind her and took hold of both of her wrists. Saya's shoulders hitched in surprise, and I spoke into her ear.

"Are you ready? I'm going to channel some wind magic into your wand. Remember how it feels."

"W-with my body?"

"Yes, with your body." I nodded, and for some reason, her ears were bright red. "Okay, here we go—"

There, like that.

We practiced until the sun went down on the third day, and Saya completely failed to master wind magic.

Somehow she got even worse after I channeled my magic through her... How is that possible? I don't understand.

Obviously, I wasn't attending to Saya constantly. Around midday, I went off by myself and flew around town searching for my brooch, talking to as many different people as I could.

The task was to just keep asking and asking.

Of course, it's not like I expected to find information so easily, and in the end everyone I asked shook their heads and gave the same answer: "I don't know."

"I saw a brooch," said an older woman who looked like she was very experienced with magic. Looking closer, I could see she was wearing a star-shaped brooch of her own over her breast. However, it looked almost as old as she was, and it was quite worn and battered besides.

Oh, it seems like I can expect something out of her. I'm not sure what that "something" is, though...

"Wh-where did you see it?!" I latched onto this news immediately.

The woman let out a very witchy laugh. "Hee-hee-hee... Hmm, I wonder..."

"Please tell me, you wonderful woman!"

"Hee-hee-hee." Suddenly, she was shoving the palm of her hand at me.

"...What does that mean?"

"How much is this information worth to you? Hmm?"

She just stood there with her hand extended toward me. I could read the gesture now: *"If you want to hear more, pay up."*

...She plays dirty. I'd expect nothing less from a witch...

"......" I silently produced a coin from my purse and dropped it into the woman's hand. When I did, she began moving again, like a windup doll come to life.

"What I saw was—"

The woman's lengthy story only confirmed my suspicions.

O

It was my fifth night in this country.

As I was gazing up from my bed at the moon hanging in the sky outside the window, the door suddenly opened. I looked up and saw Saya staring at me timidly.

"Um, Miss Elaina?"

"What is it?"

"C-can I sleep in here with you?"

I looked down at the bed.

......

"It's a bit small, don't you think?"

"We run a cheap inn, sorry."

Ah, no, that's not what I meant. This is a one-person room. And the bed is also meant for one person to sleep in. Alone. "Well, if you don't mind being cramped, I guess it's fine with me."

"Yippee!"

Saya slammed the door shut and came into the room, then crawled into the bed. She smelled nice, as if she had just gotten out of the bath. Since this was an inn, we must have been using the same shampoo, but the scent was completely different from mine. I grabbed a bit of my hair and brought it close to my nose, but that tender, girlish fragrance wasn't coming from me.

How come she's the only one who smells so good? ...Oh well. Time for bed.

I lay down, still gazing at the moon, and drew up the covers. Soon I felt the presence of someone behind me.

"Isn't the moon too bright to look at while you're going to sleep?"

"Somewhat." I rolled over. When I did, my gaze met hers. "...Um, what was it you just said about the moon?"

"I don't mind, it's not too bright for me." She smiled slightly. In the moonlight, her smile seemed ephemeral, as if it would dissolve if I touched it.

"Good work today. You've made big improvements compared to when you first started. Soon you won't need my help at all."

"What? That's not true. There are still so many things that I want you to teach me, Elaina."

"...I'm a traveler. Before long, I'm going to leave this country."

"But we're going to be together until then."

I noticed her squirming and wriggling around under the blanket, and then something cool was on top of my hand.

She gazed into my eyes and squeezed my hand. "Please, I want you to teach me so much more."

"......"

Her eyes reflected the light of the moon.

This naive little girl must truly idolize people like me. I know I'm about to do something cruel—but then, I have to do what's best for myself.

I wasn't sure if the prickly feeling in my chest was guilt or disappointment, but I wanted to believe it was the former.

"There's no point in continuing this conversation, Saya," I said, shaking off her hand. "So why don't you give me back my brooch?"

○

The truth behind the mysterious disappearance of the brooch had turned out to be really quite simple.

"There was a young girl who ran into you, right? After you flew off in a hurry, she picked up the brooch."

Her eyes still glittering with the money I'd given her, the old woman told me she'd seen it all happen. And her story was the truth; a part of me had suspected the same thing. To not find it after searching around so thoroughly…someone must have picked it up.

I'd suspected something was up from the start.

……

Saya.

Your broom control was almost too *bad—enough to make me think that you were flying badly on purpose. After all, if you couldn't fly your broom well enough, you wouldn't even be allowed in this country.*

At first, I had assumed that Saya was a local, but when I asked her about it, she said she was a mage from an eastern country who had come here under special circumstances. If that was true, it was even stranger that she couldn't fly her broom. And so…

…Here's the truth. I doubted you from the very beginning. I waited and waited for you to give my brooch back. "But you hid it and never gave it back to me. Instead, you said you wanted me to stay with you forever. I've had it up to here with you," I told her.

Saya sat on the bed, hanging her head. I wondered what emotion was on her face, but I made no move to comfort her by touching her shoulder like I did when we first met. Unfortunately, I'm not that kind.

She kept her gaze to the ground as if to avoid the moonlight, and I simply waited for her reply.

I wonder how much time passed. One minute? Ten minutes? It might have been only ten seconds.

"…question me?"

I could just barely hear a very small voice. "What was that?" I asked.

"…Why didn't you question me?" This time I heard her clearly.

"Because I didn't have any proof. That's the first reason. Even if I accused you and called you a thief, if you had denied it, I wouldn't have had any evidence. My hands would've been tied."

"......"

"Plus, I believed you'd give it back eventually. I don't really think you're a bad person, Saya."

This innocent, high-spirited girl reminded me of a child who had been spoiled by her mother.

"So I waited," I told her.

Saya finally raised her head. Her pretty face was a mess, wrinkled up to cry. She wiped at her tears and tried to suppress her sobs as she said, "I was lonely."

"I'm not your little sister."

"I know that. I know that, but...I...I wanted to be with you." Her voice had grown so small. I wasn't sure whether she was talking to her sister or to me.

If I were to write out what I'd learned about Saya in the short time since we met, it would be an awfully short list, but somehow, I believed I had come to understand what kind of person she was. She was a useless older sister who always let her sweet younger sister indulge her. I'm sure she had always been that way, which was why she couldn't stand it when her little sister left her behind.

"I hated being alone. I hated it, and I was scared, so I—"

"Hey." I flicked her forehead, and it made a firm *twik*. "That's no excuse."

If you hate being alone, find someone to rely on. If you hate being ridiculed for being alone, get out there and find someone you get along with. If solitude is scary, do everything you can to escape it.

"Does it really matter if you're by yourself now? If you're feeling alone? Can you become an apprentice witch while you're still holding on to those fears? Whenever humans are really, seriously trying to accomplish anything, they're always alone. You can't get anything done if you're not by yourself. It's all over if you have a partner."

Your younger sister was probably trying to teach you that by leaving you. I can't say for sure, though.

"...But."

"Ah-ah-ah. No buts. I won't hear any excuses." I covered my ears with both hands and shook my head. *No way.* My hair flew around wildly and hit her in the face.

Whoops, bet she didn't like that.

"Sure, struggling by yourself is hard. It's scary. I understand that. And that's why…" As I was speaking, I used magic to conjure up a pointy hat, exactly the same as mine, and plopped it on her head. "…I'm giving you this. Let me leave a little part of myself by your side. Then you'll be all right even when you're alone."

Gripping the brim of the hat tightly, Saya said, "But if I take this, you won't have…"

"Ah, it's okay. That's a spare."

I produced another hat and showed it to her before donning it myself. "Now we match. From now on, you'll be on your own, but never truly alone. Your sister and I are always watching over you." *So give me back my brooch*, I silently urged her.

She pulled the hat way, way down on her head and gripped it very, very tightly, and with trembling shoulders, she gave a silent nod. She looked so weak and helpless.

I hugged her thin shoulders and pulled her closer.

©Azure

The day had come.

We had spent my final night in the country together. I had comforted Saya as she wept, given her some advice for passing the practical magical skills exam, heard all about the country she and her sister were from, discussed my future travels, and so on.

Oh, and it turns out that Saya is actually a very powerful mage. I mean, I had known that all along, but I never did learn why she was so bad at wind magic. On that point, no matter how much I inquired, Saya only blushed bright red and refused to answer. *What's her deal?*

At the end of it all, we had fallen asleep together just as the sun was rising. It had been a long, long night.

But a precious memory.

○

I thought back on it several months after I had left the Country of Mages.

Six months, to be exact.

About half a year has passed since I met that girl, lost my brooch, and got it back—wow, time sure does fly. Truly.

I had traveled to another country so far away that people would ask, "Huh? Country of Mages? Where's that?"

The reason I was reminiscing was that I happened to catch sight of her name as I was browsing through a bookstore.

Apprentice Witch Advancement Exam Pass List

Printed on a sheaf of really cheap-looking straw paper was the newspaper put out every month by the mysterious organization known as the United Magic Association, which was responsible for conducting the apprentice witch advancement exams, among other things. The results for the exams given all over the world, plus a few words from the passing candidates, were displayed on the front page.

Her name was there.

"Hey, no reading in the store." The shop owner appeared from the back and yanked away the newspapers.

"...Ah—" *But I wanted to keep reading.*

"You wanna read? You gotta pay."

"How much?"

"One copper."

I paid, then stuck the paper under my arm and went back to my inn, humming all the way. I pulled my chair up to the window and continued reading. In the article, the girl talked about her most difficult days and her hopes for the future.

According to the article, she had moved to the Country of Mages with her little sister several years ago. Her sister—and only her sister—quickly became an apprentice witch and returned to their hometown without her. Then she met a certain traveler who gave her the courage to fight on her own, as well as one incredibly stylish hat. She attempted the exam many times after the traveler had left, but it proved too difficult. However, she kept trying and never gave up, and eventually, finally, she earned the rank of apprentice witch. Now she was going to return home, with plans to train hard and become a witch.

I couldn't help but smile.

Her very long story concluded with one sentence: "After I return home and become a full-fledged witch, I'd like to pay a visit to my favorite traveler."

I put the newspaper down on the desk and looked up at the sky. Somewhere out in the endless expanse of that clear, pale-blue sky, she was there.

"I'll be waiting for you—Saya."

CHAPTER 2

A Girl as Sweet as Flowers

It was the start of an in-between season, not quite spring, not quite summer.

Cutting through the cool, dry air, I flew among the broad-leaved trees of a forest. The forest seemed to be quite expansive; I'd been making my way through for some time now, but there was no end in sight.

As I wove my broom right and left to dodge the trees overhanging the extremely narrow path, the pesky branches kept rubbing against me.

I couldn't see the sky from where I was. Far off in the distance, I could just barely make out something sparkling on the other side of the mesh of green. The trees were too overgrown for me to see anything more.

"…Whoopsie."

Because I had been looking up instead of ahead, a tree branch had snatched my pointy hat. I stopped, went back, retrieved it, and then was on my way through the cramped forest again.

These woods are so dense. I should've just flown over them, I thought regretfully, but it was already too late. I had come far enough that doubling back now would take too much time. I could try to force my way up and out, but I had a feeling my hat wouldn't be the only casualty.

Somehow, it felt like I was always running late these days. As for whose fault that was, it was…well, completely mine, but so what? I kept on flying, mentally complaining to no one in particular.

I don't know how far it was, but after a while, the path suddenly opened up.

"Whoa...," I murmured.

There in the clearing was a field of flowers.

As I approached, I saw flowers of red, blue, yellow, and other hues spread out below me. Every one of them was standing tall and proud, reaching for the sun. When the breeze from my broom brushed past the blossoms, petals scattered into the wind along with a refreshing aroma.

The fragrance, sweet enough to cleanse the depths of my soul, wafted up as the vibrantly colored blossoms danced in the breeze. Holding my hat with one hand so it wouldn't fly off, I slowed my broom.

Here was a whole other world in the middle of the forest. My heart was captivated.

"...Oh my."

Among the field of vivid colors, I saw a human form.

I wonder if that's the caretaker of this place? I turned my broom in that direction.

"Um, excuse me?"

When I called out from atop my broom, the person remained seated but turned to face me. She was a lovely girl about my age. "Oh, hello."

"Hello. Are you the caretaker?"

She shook her head. "No. There is no caretaker here. I'm just here because I like the flowers."

"No caretaker...? You mean these flowers are wild?"

"Yes, that's right."

Wow.

I had thought flower fields only grew under the supervision of humans. Although I suppose flowers existed before humans did, so it's not like they needed us to grow. But to think such amazing scenery could exist just by the power of nature, without a helping human hand...

Incredible.

"Are you a witch?" Noticing my chest, the girl tilted her head.

"Indeed. I'm on a journey."

"How wonderful— Oh, actually, in that case, I have a request."

"Sure, if it's something I can do."

The girl picked a number of flowers, removed her jacket, wrapped it around them, and held them out to me. It was an impromptu bouquet. "If it's all right, I'd like you to take this bouquet to the country you're going to."

"Is there someone you want me to give them to?" I asked in confusion as I accepted the bouquet.

"No one in particular. I only ask that they be given to someone who can appreciate their beauty. That much is important."

Meaning, I suppose, that you want to spread the word about this flower field.

I certainly understood the desire to show this beautiful vista to someone.

"In other words, you want me to advertise the flower field, right?"

"Do you not want to?"

"No, I don't mind at all. In fact, I'm more than happy to," I replied.

The girl smiled with deep relief and said, "Thank goodness."

For a short while after that, we engaged in light but lively conversation. At least, I think we did. I told her about the places I had visited so far, and she told me about her favorite flowers.

After we had passed some pleasant time together, I said, "Well then, I'm going to continue on, so I'll give your flowers to someone in the next country, okay?"

"I'm counting on you, Miss Traveler." She shook my hand with a smile.

"......"

Something felt strange. "You can't leave this place, can you?"

"No, I can't," she told me plainly. "I'm fine, really, as long as I stay here in this flower field. I spend all day with the flowers. I'm happy just being here in the sunlight. Isn't it wonderful?"

The girl never got up from her spot.

○

"Stop right there, missy. Hey, I said stop!"

I had flown my broom several hours from the flower field and arrived at another country when a guard in black clothing came out to greet me in a less-than-welcoming tone of voice.

He has no reason to yell at me like that, and why's he calling me "missy"?! Even the most good-natured person in the world would have a hard time being treated this way. Naturally, I got a bit angry.

However, I didn't let it show. I'm an adult, after all.

"You a traveler?"

"Yes. Can't you can tell by looking at me?"

"What's with that bouquet?"

"Oh, it's nothing really."

"......"

"What?"

"Lemme see it." He pushed toward me and snatched the bouquet from my hands.

"Wha—? Hey!" Enough was enough, and I wasn't about to let him treat me this way. I got down from my broom, grabbed ahold of the flowers, and tried to take them back. But the guard brushed my hands aside and stared so hard at the flowers you'd think he was trying to burn a hole through them. My protests had no effect.

To make matters worse, the man just grimaced and muttered, "Wait a minute... Are these from—?" but I had no idea what he was on about.

...This guard is such a jerk.

"Where did you get these?" he asked.

"What does it matter? Give them back."

"Don't tell me you picked them up in a flower field?"

"What business is it of yours?" *You're really underestimating me, you know. How should I go about punishing you? Perhaps I should reduce you to ashes.* I pulled out my wand.

"Hey, what're you doing?"

I was getting ready to fire off a gust of wind when I heard a new voice behind me—and this one had even more authority behind it.

What the heck? Is this country just full of macho guys with big attitudes? I turned around, fuming.

"That belongs to the traveler. Give it back."

Standing there was a middle-aged man dressed in the same black clothing as the young guard. He was glaring not at me, but at his young colleague.

I turned back to the younger guard to find him gripping the flower bouquet and clearly upset at being caught. "But, sir, this…this is…"

"I'll know when I look at it. I'll handle the rest, so stand down."

"No, this is—"

"Stand. Down. Didn't you hear me? Go take a break."

"…*Tch.*" The young guard clicked his tongue, and after shooting me another nasty look, he turned to leave.

"Ah, my bouquet, if you would."

"……"

The young guard turned back, radiating protest with his entire body. "…Here." He shoved the flowers back at me.

"Thank you kindly."

He didn't answer, but he did finally leave. Every single thing he did was irritating. I was glad to be rid of him.

If we ever met again, he wouldn't be so lucky next time.

After confirming that the younger guard was no longer in sight, the older guard who had been addressed as "sir" turned to me with an apologetic expression. "My apologies, Madam Witch. His younger sister recently went missing, and he's been acting this way ever since. Please forgive him."

"It didn't bother me that much." A lie, obviously.

"Anyway, as for those flowers… I'm sorry, but would you please let me dispose of them? Bringing them into this country is strictly forbidden."

"Forbidden? Like, these flowers specifically?"

I didn't understand what he meant or what he was trying to accomplish. Unconsciously, I hugged the flowers tightly.

"Those flowers are cursed," he said matter-of-factly, without trying to pull them out of my hands. "They're harmless to a witch like you, but apparently they contain a spell that drives nonmages mad. I don't know all the details, but that's the information we have now."

"...Cursed?"

He nodded. "People who fall for those flowers are led to where they grow, then become their food. They're never seen again. That's why the flowers are forbidden."

"......"

"Is something wrong?"

"...No."

If we assume there really is a curse on these flowers—and I suspect that might be the case—why didn't the girl who gave me this bouquet try to stand up even once? And why was she sitting in the flower field? I'd been puzzling over these points the entire time.

What if it wasn't that she didn't *stand up, but that she* couldn't *stand up? What if the lower half of her body was no longer hers?*

......

"Um, about that young guard's little sister..."

"Oh. Several days ago, she went into the forest where the flowers grow, and she hasn't been seen since."

He lowered his gaze. He was looking at the bouquet. "Say, miss... did someone give those to you? Perhaps—"

"No." I interrupted him. "I gathered these myself. The clothing wrapped around the flowers is one of my spare shirts." *So I don't know anything about the guard's sister.*

I cut off his questioning with a shameless lie.

○

After that, I entered the country and found that there wasn't much in the way of sightseeing, so I headed for an inn. I rented a room for only one night, took a bath, and slid under the covers.

Staring up at the cheap wooden planks of the ceiling, I deliberated about the flower field, and about the girl sitting there.

There was a book I had read a long time ago, *The Adventures of Niche*, in which there had been a story about another strange plant. As I recall, in one part of that story, there was a plant with a mutation that caused it to absorb magical energy rather than exude it the way normal plants did. It gained sentience and eventually became violent.

First, I should clarify that the substance we know as "magical energy" flows freely from every part of the natural world. Flowers, trees, and other flora especially produce and exude magical energy by absorbing sunlight. Honestly, I don't really understand the theory behind it all.

Anyway, the human body is typically unable to absorb this energy, but there are certain people who can harness it regardless, and even use it at will. We call them mages.

That's why our powers can reach their full potential in the middle of a forest overflowing with raw magical energy. When I was still studying to be a witch, the place where my teacher trained me was also a forest.

You could say that we mages resemble the mutated plant in *The Adventures of Niche*. We have become able to handle things that humans ordinarily can't.

…Or is it that people who can't *do magic are the rare ones?*

I don't know which is which. I feel like it might not be a good idea to think too deeply about these things. Plus, sitting and trying to puzzle it out doesn't amount to much in the end. It's like trying to logic out which came first, the chicken or the egg. Completely unproductive.

"*…Yawn.*" I covered my mouth and rubbed my eyes. *I'm not tired yet. I'm fine. Not tired, not tired—the flower field.*

Maybe the flower field had evolved in a strange way because there was *too* much magic. Like the sentient plants in the story. Thinking about it, the forest around the flower field was so overgrown with trees, you couldn't see the sun through the foliage. The magical energy produced in such a place could create the necessary conditions.

It wouldn't really be so strange for the flower field to mutate due to the great overabundance of magical energy.

And so the flower field began to draw humans in with whispers of nectar-sweet poison. What on earth had been born there?

"……"

What had become of the humans lured to that flower field?

A bad feeling took root in my mind, and I couldn't shake it.

O

"Hello again, Madam Witch. Leaving already?"

It was the following morning, and the older guard I'd met the previous day was standing at the border gate. It seemed that he remembered me, and he greeted me with a cheerful smile.

I returned his smile and said, "Yes. It wasn't a very large country, so I saw everything I wanted to in a day."

"Yeah…this place isn't the most exciting."

"Not at all. It was very enjoyable."

"Ha-ha, thanks for the laugh." He saw right through me.

"By the way, what happened to the young guard from yesterday?"

"Hmm? He's off today. He left the country last night and hasn't come back yet. Did you have unfinished business with him?"

"Just another joke." *I asked because I'm trying to avoid him.*

"Anyway, he said he would be coming back this evening, so you can wait if you want to see him."

"It's fine."

"Mm. So you're going, then?"

"Yes. I'm not in any particular hurry to get to the next place, but if

I don't leave the country where I'm staying in the morning, I can't usually reach the next one before sunset." *Plus, there's a stop I want to make.*

I was more concerned with that place than anything here.

"Is that so? Well, take care of yourself."

"Will do. Thanks."

And so I stepped through the gate.

Then…I could see the forest in the distance. I looked toward the area I had come from the day before and took off on my broom.

A few scattered trees led the way, as if they had been flung from the forest, lending a different hue to the sea of green spreading out before me. The cool wind blew wildly, twisting me around and chilling the earth. Clouds hung in the air, blocking out the sunlight. The gray sky had already begun to turn the color of lead.

It's going to rain soon.

O

In the forest, I avoided the creaking trees that brushed at my shoulders and found the clearing.

There was the flower field.

It looked as gloomy as the sky, and the faded colors were completely different from the vibrant tableau of the day before.

"……"

And the flowers were not only the wrong colors, but the wrong shapes as well.

As far as I knew, I had retraced my path from the day before, so I shouldn't have ended up in a place that looked so different despite its similarities. However, there was a certain uneasiness that I couldn't shake.

I got down from my broom and walked over to the source of my unease. My foot made an unsettling *squish* when it touched down, and I could feel the flower petals dying underfoot.

A pleasant scent hung in the air above the flower field.

In front of me was a person. The true source of my discomfort was there—she *was* the discomfort.

"......"

It was the young girl who had given me the flower bouquet, and now there was a man facing her, too. He was wearing different clothes from yesterday, but I remembered his face. He was sitting in the flower field, smiling at the girl.

It was the young guard.

"Hello again."

"Ah, the traveler from yesterday. Hello." He gave me a very simple reply.

"Is that...thing your little sister?" I asked.

He tilted his head. "Yes, I finally found her. I couldn't believe she was in a place like this." Still wearing a gentle expression, he grasped the girl's hand.

The longer I looked, the stranger it became—somehow, I couldn't call the girl holding the young man's hand human anymore. Flecks of green dotted her skin, ivy vines curled around her body, and her vacant eyes stared into the stagnant air without blinking. Her mouth was gaping wide like a cave, and drool oozed out from the corners.

The strangest thing, though, was her lower half. From the waist down, she was wrapped in huge red flower petals, as if a human had grown out of an enormous flower. Flower and human had become a single, bizarre sight.

The guard gazed at her, spellbound. "She's so pretty. Who would have thought she was all the way out here, becoming so beautiful?"

"......"

"What's wrong?"

I shook my head, "It's nothing. I'm just surprised because she looks very different from yesterday."

"Ah, yesterday. I'm sorry about all that. I was just feeling out of sorts because I didn't know where my sister had gone."

I turned my gaze slightly downward and saw his leg had ivy coiling around it. I'm sure he couldn't move any more than his sister could. Or rather, he *could*, but he had probably lost any desire to move.

"......"

He paid my presence no heed. If I didn't speak to him, he would soon turn back toward her and continue talking to her with vacant eyes.

"...I can't believe you kept this amazing place all to yourself."

"...Ah, that's right. Say, why don't we bring everyone here from back home? If we show them, they'll be so happy."

"...I especially want them to see you, now that you're so beautiful."

"...Hey, that's okay, right?"

"...I see. Thank you."

I suspected he was hearing words I couldn't. To me, it just looked like a one-sided conversation with the thing that used to be his sister.

The little sister had been able to converse with me the day before, but now she couldn't even blink anymore. She certainly couldn't express anything verbally. Her emotions, her physical body, her entire self had been lost in the flower field somewhere. She had lost the ability to do anything except be admired.

Just like a flower.

O

I flew over a field of grass.

Luckily, by the time I remounted my broom, the rain had stopped. *I'd like to get to the next country before it starts to rain again, but we'll see about that.*

"...Oh no."

Beneath the ashen sky, I saw something moving in the direction I was headed. As I got closer, and the blurry form grew clearer, I could tell it was a person. Without slowing down, I passed by them.

"......"

I couldn't tell whether it was a man or a woman. Their age was a mystery. I could tell only that they were human. The person was walking along to some unknown destination; if they continued straight ahead, maybe they would eventually reach another country.

All of their features had vaguely blurred together except for one thing, something they were carefully cradling in both hands. I had seen clearly what it was, but I wished I hadn't.

They carried a bouquet of flowers.

CHAPTER 3

On the Road: The Tale of a Muscleman Searching for His Little Sister

SHORTCUT STARTS HERE

There was a signboard right there, so I followed it obediently. The road was too narrow—in fact, it wasn't much of a road at all, more like a simple trail—so I couldn't use my broom. I could have insisted on flying if I'd really wanted to, but I didn't want to deal with the constant twisting and turning.

With no other option left to me, I walked along the unpaved road that wasn't a road, trampling grass underfoot. The grass, damp with morning dew, flung water droplets at me as I pressed on. The hem of my robe was already weighed down with moisture.

This might be a shortcut if you're walking, but I'm using a broom, so this is obviously a longer way around. Shoot.

Anyway…I wonder what kind of place the next country will be.

Trade must not have been big there, if this path was so undeveloped. *Meaning a country just as undeveloped as this forest. Well, that's just my guess. Hmm… Suddenly my desire to go there had vanished. Let's turn back, shall we?*

Just joking.

I walked on for some time, complaining all the while in my head. Finally, a change appeared in the otherwise uniform forest scenery.

"…Oh my."

A tree had fallen—a big one, maybe several hundred years old by the look of it. And it wasn't the only one lying wearily on its side; there were a whole bunch.

Whoa. What a roadblock.

However, I could still proceed onward. I crossed over the fallen trees, spreading out both arms as if I was walking a tightrope, then caught sight of a black shape moving in the shadows of the forest.

Oh, a bear?

O

Alas, it was just a human.

A giant one, with rippling muscles. Scary.

"I knocked down all the trees around us with my own two hands. How about that? Pretty impressive, huh?"

With a grunt, he struck a pose to show off his muscles. Plenty of people could fell trees with raw strength, but I kept that thought to myself.

"Would you happen to be a resident of the country up ahead?"

He spoke while taking a different pose. "That's right. I come from that country. How did you know? Could you tell from my muscles?"

"Huh? Do you mean to say that your homeland is full of musclemen like you?" *Maybe I should turn back.*

"No, not at all. They're all scrawny little bean sprouts there."

"What were you trying to say, then?"

"Doesn't matter. How about these muscles?"

I don't think I'm going to get very far with this guy. I tried to humor him. "Oh, what amaaazing muscles. Can I feel them?"

"Go right ahead!" The huge man offered his arm to me with another grunt and flexed.

I didn't really know how best to touch it, so I tried poking it with my index finger. "Wooow, amazing." It was as hard as a rock.

"……"

"Um, why are you turning red?"

"…Forgive me. It's the first time any girl has ever touched me, other than my little sister, so…"

By that logic, do you mean you're fine with your sister touching your arms? I see. Seriously, what's with that twisted rationale? Go die.

After shaking off my dark thoughts, I asked, "By the way, what are you doing out here in the forest? Are you working?"

"No, I'm actually in training right now."

And then he told me his story.

A few days earlier, his younger sister had been kidnapped by a strange group. The muscleman hadn't been around, and so he hadn't been able to rescue her.

He had heard from an eyewitness that the people who kidnapped his sister were a bunch of burly men. In order to take them on, he had taken up training here and knocked down all the trees one by one.

…And he had also incidentally taken a part-time job as a lumberjack to make money.

"…So you're just knocking trees down for money, then?"

"What are you saying? Making money isn't the point. I need more muscle—so much more," he denied with heaving breaths. Something about this was strange.

"Isn't your goal to rescue your younger sister?"

"That'll happen sooner or later. I don't have enough muscle to fight the burly men who kidnapped her."

Um, you're already superhuman, so please go ahead and save your sister already.

…It seemed like I might meet the same fate as the fallen trees if I said that aloud, though, so I just gave an exaggerated nod.

"First of all," he continued, "I've got to take down the champion of this forest—the bear. This is my first objective."

"A bear…?"

"Yes. A scary one, too. He can grab fish out of the river with his bare paws. I'm nowhere near that dexterous."

"Uh-huh…"

"After that, they say there's an ax-wielding oddball living deep in the forest, and I have to duel him, too. I've heard that he wrestled the bear to the ground. He's one to be feared."

"Uh-huh…"

If the bear has already been defeated in a wrestling match, then hasn't it already lost its "champion of the forest" title?

"After that—"

He made me listen to his plans for about an hour, but the words *little sister* never once came out of his mouth. I had to wonder if he really had any intention of going to help her. Maybe his overtrained muscles had started constricting the blood flow to his brain. He'd completely lost sight of his original goal. In the end, rescuing his little sister had become less and less important.

I wonder when he'll remember why he's doing all this in the first place.

Well, that story has nothing to do with me.

CHAPTER 4

Fund-Raising

"...Ah, this is bad."

I had arrived at a small country that didn't seem to have any defining characteristics, but I wasn't lamenting the clichéd townscape. My purse, on the other hand, was in terrible shape.

After I was forced to sacrifice three silver coins for the entrance fee, the remaining three coppers and single silver coin had to huddle together into a pitiful little quartet. Sadly, the silver coin was so old and tarnished, you couldn't distinguish it from the coppers at all if you didn't look closely. I wasn't sure if I'd be able to use it.

A copper coin was usually enough to buy one loaf of bread. With a silver coin, you could get one night at a cheap inn, and if you had gold, you could buy some high-class accessories.

Which meant the best I could do right now would be to sink my teeth into some bread at a drafty old inn, curl up beneath some thin sheets, and try to sleep away the hunger pangs. That was about it.

In short, I was close to death.

"...What am I going to do?"

I always feel most like spending money when I'm having money problems. Holding my grumbling stomach, I walked along a large avenue. Food stalls were lined up like sparkling jewels, selling bread, fruits, vegetables, and more. Famished as I was, I could almost hear them calling to me.

Ah, I want to eat everything...

I want to eat—

"Um, I'd like some bread, please."

When I came to, I was standing in front of a food stall. The rich scent of wheat wafted through the air. There were no prices listed.

The good-natured older woman seated on the other side of the tray of bread looked at me and smiled. "That'll be three coppers."

Oh, the nerve. Coming here was a mistake.

Turned out she was an old bat who extorted money from the poor.

"Hmm? Please excuse me; maybe my hearing isn't so good anymore. Could you say that once more, please?"

"That'll be three coppers."

"I see, so three pieces of bread cost three coppers?"

"The price is for one, obviously. Something wrong with your head, missy?"

I should be asking the same thing! Are you stupid? Why should I have to turn over three copper pieces for some stale bread that's been left out for who knows how long? I wanted to let her have it with one of the several complaints that came to mind, but unfortunately, I didn't have the energy to raise my voice.

In the end, I said nothing and left. Still exhausted and sustained by nothing but air and my own saliva, I passed by the awful food stalls that were tempting me.

Proceeding straight down the broad avenue, I came to an open square where a large fountain stretched up toward the sky. There was nothing unusual about it; it was the kind of architecture you might see anywhere. And on the bench next to the fountain sat a man and woman chatting and laughing, paying no mind to their surroundings—another completely ordinary scene.

......

I decided not to dwell on whether my irritation actually justified the desire to roast them alive and headed toward the fountain instead. Scooping up the running water with both hands, I drank. The cold liquid ran down my throat, and I felt instantly refreshed.

"Oh, look, darling, that witch is drinking the fountain water."

"She really is! How uncouth! Ha-ha-ha-ha!"

"......" I gathered magical energy in my hands, pulled out my wand, and turned around silently.

Instantly, with a subtle *crack*, the bench split in two.

"Kyah! What on earth happened to the bench?"

"Maybe it's jealous of our love! Ha-ha-ha!"

"......"

They were so stupid, I couldn't even be mad at them anymore.

The fountain water had soothed my empty stomach somewhat, so after putting my wand away, I continued on.

First of all, I had to find a place to spend the night.

○

"You want to rent a room? That'll be three silver coins."

"For three nights, yes? Sorry, I only want to reserve one night."

"No, one night is three silvers."

"......"

This was already the sixth inn. I had started my search with the cheapest-looking hotels, so how was this happening? Every single inn was at least three times the usual price.

This place had cracks in the walls and didn't even have a bath, but the proprietor was saying that one night cost three silver coins? What a joke.

I kept at it. "Can't we negotiate? I only have one silver and three coppers..." I turned my purse upside down on the counter. *Clink*—you could hear the sad truth.

"Isn't that only four coppers?"

"Ah, this one's silver."

"...Oh, so it is. It's very dirty."

"Isn't there anything you can do?"

"There's nothing I can do." The man running the inn sighed. "Please understand, miss. This is a business."

"So extorting money from the poor is a business?"

"Commerce has always been this way."

"Aughhh…" There was no denying that, and it looked like staying at this inn was not an option. "I have a question for you."

"What is it?"

"Don't you think that the prices in this country are a little too high? The town doesn't even have any sights to see or any unique local product that would justify raising all the basic consumer prices so much."

"Uh… Miss, you're a traveler, so you wouldn't know…," the innkeeper murmured.

As I expected, there was more to it.

After glancing around, the innkeeper lowered his voice. "The newly crowned king is a foolish man, and he artificially inflated the local currency."

"Artificially? Do you mean counterfeit money is circulating through the market?"

The innkeeper nodded. "Indeed. And with all the counterfeit money going around, the value of our currency crashed. As an outsider, the prices in this country would seem a little high, but for everyone who lives here, everything's a reasonable price."

"Reasonable, hmm…? But it's counterfeit money, right? Isn't there any penalty for using it?"

"The king's the one who put it into the market, so I should hope not."

I see.

I finally understood what was going on in this country. I didn't know what the king was trying to do, but if he thought he could stimulate his economy with counterfeit currency, he must be bona fide fool. However, there apparently hadn't been much pushback from his citizens about it…

"It doesn't really matter if the money we're using is real or fake. If the king increases the amount of money in circulation, the citizens can just increase prices. It doesn't cause problems for us locals. Only travelers like you run into trouble."

"...We sure do. People coming from outside are liable to have their hearts broken by the high prices." *People like* me.

The innkeeper glanced quickly at something behind me. When I looked, another customer had lined up behind me, and I saw the three silver coins for one night. Apparently, paying triple the ordinary price really did seem appropriate to the locals.

"Will that be all, miss?"

"Yes. Thank you very much for your valuable information."

I bowed and left the inn.

O

I would have to work to earn money for a room.

I went back to the broad avenue where I had failed to buy bread and sat unobtrusively on the side of the road to watch the people walking by. They seemed so carefree, going about their shopping.

Even knowing that they were using counterfeit money, they were happy as could be.

"......"

Since I was a traveler, sooner or later I was bound to use up all of my money. I had never settled down somewhere and taken a job, so it was inevitable. I had run into cash problems many times before now. I couldn't even enter a new country if I ran out of money, after all.

Normally, I would pretend to be a shopkeeper, or help out someone in need, or do something else to earn a little pocket change. *But,* I thought, *if it doesn't matter whether the money people are using is real or fake, then there's no reason not to use that to my advantage, is there?*

This time I'll sell my services at three times the usual price, too. Then I'll be just like everyone else around here—someone who can use counterfeit currency without a shred of guilt.

"Hey, you," I called out to a young man walking down the street with a sullen expression.

His shoulders hitched in surprise, and he turned toward me. "Huh, me?"

I nodded and beckoned him over. "There's something troubling you, isn't there?"

"Um, who are you?"

"Goodness, how rude of me. I forgot to introduce myself. I am a traveling fortune-teller," I said shamelessly, then pushed up my pointy hat and stared at the sullen youth.

"Something troubling me…?" he replied, still skeptical. "Do I really look that upset?"

"Indeed. It's the only emotion I see on your face."

"Really…"

"Truly." I nodded vigorously.

In my experience to date, when it comes to business dealings, hesitation is directly connected to failure. The moment you show hesitation—the moment a crack becomes visible—that's when the other party starts to be suspicious of you. In other words, it's best to act with confidence.

That's why I promptly asserted, "Quite often we don't know what is bothering us. For example, lack of confidence in your personal appearance, or problems at work, or feelings of dread about failing to meet our soul mate even after such a long time—"

"……!"

I spotted the slight change in his expression. *Aha, so he's having trouble finding a girlfriend. Is that it?*

"You're feeling troubled because…you cannot find a girlfriend. Isn't that right?"

"…I guess so, yeah."

He turned to look away, and I spoke again. "Shall I read your fortune and find out when your soul mate will appear before your eyes?"

I took out my wand and summoned some magical energy. With a cute *poof!* sound, a small flame appeared.

"...Ah." And immediately after it appeared, it was blown out by a breeze. Apparently, I hadn't summoned enough magical energy. Smoke drifted from the tip of my wand in a reluctant farewell.

I was supposed to examine the flames to tell a fortune, but it wasn't happening.

After blowing all the rest of the smoke out, I waved my wand around. "Ah, I see, I see."

"Huh? That was enough?"

"Yes. What I just performed is known as a smoke reading, a style of fortune-telling in which I predict your fortune by examining the smoke." A lie, of course.

"I've never heard of anything like that."

"That may well be so. This style of fortune-telling is a secret art, passed down through the generations of my family, so it's not something that most people would know about."

I couldn't afford to blow my cover, so I had to cut off the idle chit-chat. "By the way, regarding your soul mate..."

"Y-yeah. So? When can I meet her?"

"Today."

"Huh, today? Wait, are you saying it's y—?"

"This evening, your soul mate shall appear before your eyes," I continued, before he could embarrass himself and say something he would regret. "If you go straight ahead from here, there's a plaza with a fountain, right? There should be a broken bench next to the fountain." I took something out of my purse and held it out to him. "If you wrap this around your hand and stand next to the bench, your soul mate will appear before you."

He took the object from my hand and tilted his head in confusion.

"...What's this? It just looks like an ordinary piece of string."

"It most certainly is not. That is a magic string, imbued with my magical energy. It has the power to draw your fortunes to you."

I hadn't actually put any magical energy into the string, of course.

And even if I were to do so, it wouldn't have the power to draw anyone's fortunes closer. In fact, I had picked up the string earlier at one of the stalls.

"If I have this string…I'll meet my…"

"Your soul mate, yes. Now look sharp and go wait until this evening. You wouldn't want to disappoint the one you're destined for, would you?"

Somewhat puzzled, the young man gripped the string tight. "Got it. I'm going to wrap this string around my hand and wait by the bench."

He stood up to leave, wearing a renewed smile, but I stopped him immediately.

"Sir, the fee for the string and the fee for the fortune-telling come to one gold piece all together." The youth grimaced visibly, until I said the magic words: "Worry not. If by chance you do not meet the one, I shall offer you a full refund."

About an hour had passed since the gloomy-faced young man had left.

A single young woman walked by. Her dress was plain, and so was her face—everything about her was plain, really. She looked about the same age as me.

There was plenty to work with, but she was squandering her potential with clothes that looked like they came off the closet floor, to say nothing of her poor skin and hair regimen.

Just like my dull silver coin. And so my next customer had been chosen.

"Hey, you!" I called out to her as she passed by, head down. "Am I correct in assuming you are struggling to find a lover?"

The young woman jumped in surprise and turned toward me. "…M-me?"

"Yes, you."

"Um, who are you?"

"Goodness, how rude of me. I completely forgot to mention that I am a traveling fortune-teller," I said shamelessly, then pushed up my pointy hat and stared at her.

The girl trembled like prey caught in the eyes of a predator. "H-how did you know that?" she fearfully asked.

"I know these things. I am a fortune-teller, after all. I can see everything, from your troubled feelings to your fated soul mate."

"M-my soul mate? Y-you can really see that?"

"Indeed. I can see him clearly before my very eyes." Of course, it was all lies.

"Then when will he appear?"

"Today."

"T-today…?"

The girl looked at me with apprehension, her heart racing at the mention of a soul mate. But I was in no rush. Everything was proceeding exactly as planned.

"If you go straight ahead from here, there is a plaza with a fountain, right? There should be a broken bench next to the fountain." And so, keeping a very even composure, I told her the rest. "This evening, a young man with an old piece of string wrapped around his hand will appear there. He is the one."

O

Things continued in this fashion for a while.

I picked up some rocks around the area and told people they would improve their fortunes, manipulated soul mates into meeting each other, and so on. After several days of excellent business, my purse was bulging with coins. By my estimation, I had made enough to live large for several months here.

Well, well, I must give my thanks to the king who made the counterfeit coins.

Since the prices were so high in this country, I used up a lot of money on room and board, but everyone was happy to pay a much higher rate for my "services" than usual. The actual value of money in this country was lower than in other countries.

"…Yes—I have imbued this HALF-OFF sign with my magic power. If you hang it in front of your shop, bread will be flying off the shelves."

"Really? I'll try it right away."

"Is that so? Well, the fee for the sign and the fee for the consultation come to three gold pieces all together."

"Are you giving me three signs?"

"The price is for one, obviously. Something wrong with your head?"

The coins in my wallet multiplied once again.

I sold my handwritten sign to the woman from the bread shop, who had come to me after hearing rumors about my services, and with that my work was over for the day. A joyful jingling noise was coming from my very heavy wallet.

Well then, time to return to my pitiful lodgings. I stood up, stretched a bit, and collected my belongings.

"You there!"

Suddenly, someone grabbed my shoulders from behind, and I turned around in surprise. Standing there was a soldier.

Several soldiers, in fact. There were about ten of them, all dressed alike, and they slowly fanned out to surround me. Each one was holding a spear, and they had guns slung across their backs. They didn't really seem to belong here.

"You're the fortune-teller, right?" the man standing directly in front of me demanded.

"No, you're mistaken."

"Don't lie. We've been watching you interact with customers."

"……"

Sweat broke out on my cheeks.

Crap. Crap, crap, crap.

What do I do? Someone must have made a complaint about me running a scam—but it's not like I really cheated anybody. Ahhh, what do

I do now…? I can't run; they've got me surrounded. I could use magic to escape, but I don't want to make enemies of an entire country…

"Come with me," the man in front of me said dispassionately. "The king wants to meet you."

I couldn't believe my ears—but I'm sure that's no surprise.

The circle of men around me brought me through their bland city and arrived at a very bland palace. Save for the ludicrous prices, there was really nothing interesting about this country at all.

On a raised dais where two staircases met in the most spacious room in the palace, a young man sat on an expensive-looking chair between two thrones.

From his seat, the young king looked down at me and spoke. "So you are the traveling fortune-teller, hmm? You're quite young."

"You are quite young yourself, Your Majesty. I thought you would be more advanced in years." The soldiers glared at me coldly, but I hadn't meant to be snarky. I really was expecting someone older.

The king addressed the soldiers. "You can all go. Leave us," he said, brushing them away with his hand. The soldiers withdrew, leaving only the two of us in the spacious chamber, and the king spoke again. "I've heard rumors that you can actually predict the future. Is that true?"

"Yes, well…it's more accurate to say that I help the future along."

"And do your abilities only work on humans?"

"What do you mean?"

"I'm asking if it might work on a broader scale as well." His voice was quite calm. I couldn't get a read on what he was thinking at all.

Does he believe in my abilities? Or does he doubt them? Or did he see through my lies?

I skirted the question. "What kind of future do you want to know about?"

"The future of this country," the young king replied.

"The future of the country... Huh." As I was nodding obediently, I thought, *That's it?* You didn't need to be a fortune-teller to predict the future of *this* country. It was simple.

Oh well, I'm not really a fortune-teller anyway.

"Before I answer your question, there is one thing I would like to ask you, Your Majesty."

"What is it?"

"Please tell me your reasons for putting counterfeit money into your country's economy."

He knit his eyebrows and let out a sigh. "That's nonsense."

"What, it's all real money?" I thought of the coins straining my wallet. *If all of them are real, I'm outrageously rich! Yay!*

"...Yes. I put real, authentic currency into circulation—though it wasn't my idea."

"Did someone tell you to?"

The young king nodded. "There's someone who was very close to the previous king. Since I've only just ascended to the throne, I am entrusting all matters of economic policy to him. His plan was to stimulate our economy by circulating the newly minted currency, but it hasn't been going so well."

"......"

That doesn't seem like the issue here, but...

"After the sudden increase in coinage, word spread that the new money was counterfeit, but that is complete nonsense."

"...Is there no chance that this close adviser has been telling you lies?"

"No chance at all. I secretly summoned several experts to the palace and had them investigate the matter, but the newly minted coins are without a doubt the real thing. The rumor about counterfeit money is false," the young king said, then stood up.

He slowly descended the stairs from the dais and approached me.

"My adviser has really done well for this country. In fact, I think he ought to be king instead of me, though the hereditary nature of our monarchy makes that impossible. In addition to advancing govern-ment policies, he is always by my side to advise me. If he weren't here, I would have lost my crown already, I'm sure."

"......"

Coming to a stop directly in front of me, the king wore a pained expression. "But this time, I'm beginning to wonder. I don't think he is guiding us to future prosperity. I don't want to doubt him, but the current state of our economy is not good. These baseless rumors about false currency are running rampant, and now that prices are rising, travelers are staying away. Trade isn't going well, either."

After hearing his troubles, I could think of only one thing. *He wants me to reassure him.* He wanted someone to tell him the future of the country would be peaceful, that the adviser he trusted wasn't lying to him, and put his fears to rest.

He seems like a very straightforward person. No, it's probably more accurate to say that he's honest to the point of tactlessness.

"And that's why I want you to predict the future of this country. Can you do it?" he asked.

Of course, my answer was already decided.

"I can." I nodded, and the young king's eyes sparkled.

"Oh, really?!" He reached for my hand in his enthusiasm, so I pulled my hand in and took a step backward.

"Yes, I never lie," I said. *Is this what people are talking about when they say lying is as easy as breathing for some people?* "However, before I predict the future of your country, I have some conditions."

"Name them."

I put up my index finger. "First of all, allow me to stay here for one night. Fortune-telling for a whole country is a demanding job. Plus, it's necessary for me to understand the whole country from the palace that stands at its center."

"Okay. Understood. I'll arrange for it at once." The young king nodded enthusiastically.

I put up the next finger. The first condition had just been a freebie.

It wouldn't be wrong to say it was a preparatory step to assist in my actual plan. The next condition was the important one.

"And secondly…"

○

After that, I went to the room provided by the young king, lay down on a soft, fluffy bed for the first time in a long while, and reviewed my strategy. I had to wait until it was time to act.

When the sun outside my window had completely set and the sky had been painted in darkness, I opened my eyes.

It's finally time.

I took out my wand and placed the tip against my head. "Ey."

With a little *poof!* I became a small mouse.

I had cast a spell on myself to change shape. I was tired, so I didn't really want to do it, but there was no way around it. My transformation let me move about with ease as I ran toward my goal, recalling the map I had asked the young king to show me earlier.

Since there was a possibility I would meet a violent end if I went down the wrong corridor, I chose to move through the attic instead of the dazzling palace interior. I pitter-pattered along the dusty floorboards until I arrived directly above the room of the king's adviser.

Peering down through a crack in the ceiling, I could see a middle-aged man with his elbows propped up on a writing desk. A single soldier was standing at attention across from him, wearing the same uniform as the ones from that afternoon.

I could guess from the tension in the air that this wasn't a friendly chat.

"Well, how about it, Father?" the young man said.

"How about what?" The older man scratched his head. "The plan is proceeding well. Before long, it will be time to oust that king, I think."

"And when will that be? You've been saying 'before long' for a good while now." The young man's voice was strained with frustration.

Wait a second—I've heard that voice somewhere before. My tiny mouse brain tried to remember, and one person came to mind who bore a close resemblance.

I think the young man speaking with the older man is the soldier who seized me by the shoulder this afternoon. If I'm not mistaken...

"The king summoned a traveling fortune-teller to the palace, and I'm sure he asked her about the future of our country. It's likely that our plan is now known to the king."

The older man smiled. "That boy is utterly devoted to me; I doubt he would do such a thing. He probably just had her predict his luck for tomorrow."

"......"

"Besides, that traveling fortune-teller is suspicious, too. She's probably a petty con artist."

Ack.

"...The fortune-teller is just a young girl."

"Looks can be deceiving."

Yes, you're exactly right. I'm not simply a young girl, you know; I'm a witch.

Perhaps tiring of the conversation, the young man sighed heavily. "Anyway, keep your promise," he said.

"Yes, I intend to, so you carry out your part of this, too. Your actions are critical to my plan, after all."

"...I understand."

The young man was about to leave the room when it happened.

The ceiling creaked, then broke open with a loud crack and crunch, and a witch with ashen hair and a wand in her hand tumbled down into the room.

I wonder who that could be?

If you guessed me, you are correct.

"…Hah, hah, whew…"

Ahhh, I must look so uncool.

My spell had worn off halfway through my mission. *I should be more careful about attempting unfamiliar spells.*

Apparently, the ceiling was just right for a mouse to peer through a crack to look below, but not a whole human body. It broke the moment I returned to my normal shape.

Maybe it was rotten with age? Certainly not because I'm heavy… probably.

"Wh-who's that?!"

When I stood up, brushing off dust, I found that the older man had a gun trained on me. It must have been concealed in his desk.

Well, he's prepared.

I waved my wand. Instantly, a bouquet of flowers blossomed from the gun's muzzle. It was a beautiful arrangement, if I do say so myself.

"Why, you—! Th-this is…"

In my admiration for the flowers, I had forgotten all about the fact that there was another person behind me. But turning around would have been too much work. *Tonk.* I tapped the floor with my wand and gave orders to the scattered fragments of wood from the ceiling.

The fragments suddenly sprouted green vines of ivy that flew toward the two men and captured them.

"You're the king's adviser, right?" I stared at the older man, whose hands and feet were now bound.

He glared at me with confusion and hatred. "Who are you?"

"Father, this is the traveling fortune-teller," the younger man shouted from behind me.

I nodded calmly. "He's right. Traveling fortune-teller, at your service."

The older man wriggled his body like a caterpillar, completely immobile. "…What do you want with me?"

"Come now, don't you already know the answer to that?"

"……"

Silence.

I turned around. The man who had escorted me here this afternoon was glaring at me.

"What are your intentions?"

And so I answered, "I intend to predict a peaceful future for this country."

○

After that, the two men were arrested when the palace guards came to investigate the commotion. They were brought before the king and forced to spill the whole truth.

Father and son had been scheming to take over the country.

As I suspected, the new currency *had* been counterfeit. Apparently, the experts who had told the young king the currency was genuine had accepted bribes from the adviser and were dirty fakes themselves.

The two had tried to plunge the country into chaos on purpose, creating doubt about the successor to the crown. Their plan was to direct the blame onto the young king and orchestrate his fall from grace. They must have hoped the adviser could become the new king, with his son as his heir.

Well, that plan ended in failure.

Now they were locked up in jail. I didn't know what would become of them, but I didn't need to involve myself in this any further.

After the cross-examination of the two conspirators was complete, I was summoned up between the thrones to accept a gift from the young king.

"Thank you very much." I checked the contents and nodded. Inside my purse was a large number of antiquated coins.

As my second condition for predicting the future of the country, I had him exchange all the money I had earned for the old type, to rid myself of any counterfeits.

"I will exchange all the counterfeit money that circulated throughout the country." The young king sounded exhausted. "It seems the majority of the money in your wallet was counterfeit as well."

"I expected as much."

The meaning of my promise to predict the future of the country had become a bit vague. Since I had rid the young king of the real problem plaguing him, he was no longer in need of a fortune-teller.

I was relieved to find I didn't have to stretch the truth any further.

There were some things that worried me a little about what would come next for him and his people, but I would have to leave this place soon. I was a traveler, after all. As for what path this country would follow, unless someone really did look into the future, nobody would ever know. Including me, of course.

"But it is really too bad." The young king sighed deeply. "To think, he was lying to me all along."

"That's the thing about liars," I replied. "You can never see it in their face."

CHAPTER 5

On the Road: The Tale of Two Men Who Couldn't Settle a Contest

As I flew my broom over gently sloping meadows, the sound of the wind rustling through the grass reached my ears. The warm sunlight and cool breeze made a pleasant harmony. I wanted to fly around this place forever.

I steered my broom left and right, and I could hear it cut through the wind—*hyoom, hyoom*—making my ride a little more fun. But unfortunately, the fun never lasted long, and this time was no different, as a less pleasant sound on the wind brought my enjoyment to an abrupt end.

"Huh? What'd you say? Try saying that again, bro!"

"Huh? I told you, I'm the best, bro!"

The uncommonly refreshing atmosphere was spoiled.

When I turned my head to figure out where the voices were coming from, I saw two men standing in the middle of a meadow arguing about something. They were dressed in different-colored clothes, and the snippet of conversation I'd overheard told me they were brothers.

"No way, I'm better than you. Absolutely!"

"No way, of course I'm better. No younger brother has ever surpassed his older brother!"

"Ha-ha! What an outdated way of thinking. A real antique outlook. Younger brothers throughout history have grown by observing their older brothers' failings. They can avoid mistakes before they happen, and that makes them stronger."

"Ha-ha! What a stupid thing to say. That must be a story from back when older brothers were useless human beings! But I myself am already a flawless, perfect specimen! I don't make mistakes, and even supposing that I did, they would be mistakes at a level higher than you could ever reach."

The two shouted nonsensical insults at each other, glaring and yelling things like "Huh?" and "You wanna go?"

Anyway, what's an "antique outlook"? Or a "high-level mistake"? I was puzzling over this when I met the gaze of the one I assumed was the older brother.

"All right then!" he shouted. "We'll get that girl over there to tell us which one of us is better, you or me!"

The (presumably) younger brother nodded. "I like that idea. Especially because I'm going to win."

I had a very, very bad feeling about this.

"So what are you two fighting about?"

I was sitting down on the grass, looking up at the two of them. Both had the same features and the same haircut; in fact, the only difference between them was the color of their clothing. The older brother wore red, while the younger brother was in blue.

The red- and blue-clothed brothers spoke in unison. ""Magic tricks!""

"Magic tricks, is it?"

"Magic tricks!"

"I understand you, so you don't need to say it a second time."

"Magic—"

"Hey, didn't you hear her? This is why kids like you…"

"Huh? Don't act like you're better just because you were born three years before me, you jerk!"

"And *you* don't understand the difference three years makes because you're still a kid, you dumb kid."

"Oh, well, if those three years are such a big deal, then why are all your magic tricks no better than mine? Huh?"

"Would the two of you please be quiet for a minute?"

"'Kay."

"Sure."

I told them to shut up, and they did. At last, there was quiet.

Magic tricks, huh…? Being a real witch, I'm unfamiliar with sleight of hand. This is a toughie. Hmm… It's annoying when they're both talking at once, so let's have them give their sides of the story one at a time. I looked at the younger brother and asked, "Why do you perform magic tricks?"

"In our homeland, there isn't a single person who can use magic. One reason is that it's a small country, but there are also some religious reasons, not to mention a historical taboo against it."

"Hmm, hmm." I had a feeling we were about to start quite a heavy conversation.

The older brother continued the story. "But people are instinctively drawn to the forbidden, and many young people like us aspire to be mages."

"And so we thought, 'Hmm, if we pretend to be mages, couldn't we try to turn a profit?'"

"And then we hit the road, as the Nearly-But-Not-Quite-Conjurers."

Ah, this really is a heavy conversation, isn't it?

The two of them were explaining proudly and happily when I interjected, "No one got mad at you for doing that?"

The one who answered me was the one dressed in blue clothing—the younger brother. "They sure did. We even got arrested. But we weren't really using magic; it was all illusion. So no matter how many times they arrested us, they had to let us go."

"Somehow…"

I bet people saw them as heroes. I can imagine what the other members of their generation were saying, too. "The government in our country is no good! It's incompetent!" *Or something like that…*

"But did sleight of hand not get banned on account of you two?"

They gave simple answers. "Yeah, it was."

"That's why we were exiled. Now we're flat broke."

"Oh, so you were exiled?" I asked.

The two of them nodded in perfect sync.

"It's been one month since we were exiled."

"Since then, we've been working as traveling performers to make money."

"Uh-huh."

"But then we ran into a problem with our act."

"We don't have a name for it."

"A name, huh?"

"We discussed combining our names into one, as brothers, but we disagree over whose name should go first."

"And so we decided that whoever won a contest of illusions would get to be first."

I see. So that's what's going on. "And what was the outcome?"

This time it was the older brother who answered me. "As of right now...zero wins, zero losses, and fifteen ties."

"So nothing's been decided at all..."

"That's why we want you to decide a winner and loser once and for all."

"Today we put an end to the stalemate."

The two of them glared at each other, shouting, "You wanna go?" and "Huh?" and so on.

Huh? This decision is kinda serious, isn't it?

○

Their magic act was a truly incredible performance.

They pulled birds out of nowhere, caused coins to move instantly from place to place, guessed the cards I drew, and all kinds of other exciting, wondrous things.

Magic tricks are amazing.

The problem was that both of them were truly so impressive that I absolutely could not choose who was better. I realized this was one of those cases where it was impossible to decide.

"How about it? I was the most impressive, of course," the younger brother boasted.

"No way—my magic tricks were more incredible than yours. Anyone could see that," the older brother said in the same arrogant tone.

After looking back and forth between the two brothers, who were glaring at each other, I had only one thing to say: "It's a tie."

Since both brothers were remarkably talented, someone like me couldn't possibly choose a winner and a loser. That was my official stance on the matter.

To be honest, I had just gotten fed up with the whole mess. I would leave the decision to someone else, somewhere else. I was ready for the brothers to be upset with my answer, but despite their fifteen previous ties, the two of them were surprisingly calm.

"...I see. Well, that's that, then. We can't decide on a name yet."

"Come on, I'm telling you my name should go first."

"What'd you say?"

"You heard me."

"Both of you, stop it, please."

"'Kay."

"Sure."

I made them quiet down and then took a step back.

"Well then, I'll be taking my leave." *I need to hurry along to the next country; I am a traveler, after all.* With a forced smile, I started to leave.

But then—"H-hey! Wait a minute."

"Aren't you going to pay us?"

The two brothers stopped me.

Huh? Pay? "You're going to charge me for that magic show?"

I turned around, and the two brothers shrugged in unison.

"I mean, of course."

"Getting to see our incredible tricks for free would be too good to be true, right? Right?"

"Right."

What happened to the two people who had been snarling at each other until just a moment ago? The men in front of me were in perfect sync.

Suddenly, I was very uncomfortable. "Wait, you never said a single word about collecting payment..."

"I don't remember saying it was free, either," the younger brother said, snorting.

"Wait just a minute. Let's review, shall we? You two wanted me to choose the superior illusionist, and you made me become the judge in your contest. Am I correct so far?"

"Yes, that's correct." The older brother nodded.

"Okay," I continued. "That's right. Meaning this was a contest between the two of you, not a magic show you were advertising? Is there a reason to pay money for that?"

"Don't be ridiculous. Our magic tricks are always a contest between us. Right?"

"Right."

Seriously...?

They set me up. They were planning to trick me from the beginning.

Get into a fight, call a traveler over, then force her to watch your magic show and charge money... No doubt this was the sixteenth time they'd pulled their little scam. *They should be ashamed of themselves.*

"...Well, how much is the fee?" I decided to ask, just in case. It didn't mean I accepted their explanation.

"Four silver pieces."

"The two of us together comes to eight silvers."

"Whoa, that's pricey."

Since one silver was enough for one night at an inn, these two were telling me to throw away enough money for over a week of lodging. *What on earth are they thinking?*

"We showed you a first-rate traveling magic show. I'd say it's a good deal, wouldn't you?" the older brother said.

Well, I can't deny that the illusions were amazingly skillful.

"......"

I'm very, very reluctant, but unfortunately, they're not wrong. Technically, they could say it was my fault for not asking about the price, and I wouldn't be able to argue.

......

But I don't wanna pay for something this stupid, especially when they're forcing me...

I thought on and on until I was worn out.

"Stop right there." I turned around, and the giant muscleman from the other day was posing there like a hero.

What in the world...?

"Um, hi there." I gave a little bow, and he reacted a little bashfully.

"Good to see you again, Madam Witch."

"It's been a while, Muscleman."

"Muscleman" was the incredibly brawny man I had met several days ago. I had defaulted to calling him that because I had only met him once and hadn't even asked his name. He seemed to enjoy hearing the word *muscle*, and he puffed out his chest. "Hmm, that's right. I *am* a muscular man."

Wow, he looks so dumb.

Frightened by the sudden appearance of the mysterious bodybuilder, the two swindlers were visibly trembling.

"H-hey...who is that guy?"

"What? Don't tell me he's your boyfriend."

"No way." I was very clear. *Meatheads are* not *my type.*

Muscleman didn't care about my attitude in the least (actually, he probably didn't even hear what I said) and spoke to the two magicians in a booming voice.

"Anyway, you there! Even if the gods forgive you for deceiving people to earn some easy coin, I shall not. Prepare yourselves." It was hard to listen to him, in more ways than one. I turned my head away.

"…Why do you avert your eyes?" He saw me.

"Uh, no reason," I said. "By the way, why are you here, Muscleman?"

"Ah, the truth is, I was just on my way to defeat a legendary dragon that is said to live in the next country. I was running there, racing the wind, when I caught sight of you—"

"What about your sister?"

"Sister?" After he had been quiet for a moment, he said, "Ah, my sister…my sister, yes. I was just thinking I would go look for her after I defeat the legendary dragon. Ha-ha-ha!" His laughter was forced and fake and far too loud.

You obviously forgot about her.

Even his brain had turned to muscle, but that was no surprise.

"…In that case, this man has nothing to do with this, right?"

"Yeah. Nothing at all. Which is why you need to leave."

The two were startled into being overly direct. I mean, when you're suddenly confronted by a burly bruiser, it's understandable to feel a bit threatened.

"Silence!" Muscleman barked.

The two brothers squeaked in terror, and I almost burst out laughing.

"Extorting money from sweet girls like her is not something that people should be doing! We're going to whip your character into shape, starting now! Come on!" Then Muscleman grabbed the two brothers by the napes of their necks and ran off.

"Ah, hang on… Hey, that hurts! Stop it!"

"He's muscle! All muscle!"

"I'll show you the splendor of the muscle world! Bwah-ha-ha-ha!"

"Ow! Let me go! Let gooo!"

"Wahhh! I'm sorry! We won't trick people anymore!"

"Bwah-ha-ha-ha-ha-ha-ha! Ha-ha-ha-ha-ha-ha-ha!"

……

I stood in the spot where I had taken the bait, and waved good-bye to the two crying swindlers. Even when the three of them looked as small as rice grains, their pitiful wailing echoed endlessly across the sweeping meadow.

Well, that was lucky. I wonder what will become of the two brothers and the muscleman.

But of course, that wasn't any of my business.

CHAPTER 6

Bottled Happiness

Wind ran over a gently sloping meadow tinged with brilliant green. The wildflowers glimmered in the sunlight like the surface of still water, swaying in the wind.

When I looked up, there was a small cloud swimming leisurely across the sky, and I felt like I could reach out and touch it.

A single witch was flying across this captivating vista on her broom. She was in her late teens, and she wore a pointy hat and a black robe with a star-shaped brooch over her breast. There's no need to tell you who she might be— That's right. She's me.

Now, we can take the time to really appreciate this amazing scenery, but let's move the story along...

I saw a person standing all alone in the middle of the meadow. When that person caught sight of me, they waved.

They don't look hostile. I'll wave back—as elegantly as possible, of course.

"Heeey! Heeeeey!" The person was hopping up and down, waving their arms, and trying their best to call attention to themselves... *I guess they really want me to come over there.*

I changed my broom's course a little and made my way over to them.

"Yay! You came!"

When I got there, I found a young boy hugging a bottle in one arm.

"Hello there." I alighted from my broom and bowed slightly.

"Hiya! Wow, miss, you're a real witch!" The boy glanced at my brooch and then smiled.

"What are you up to?" I asked.

"I'm on a happiness hunt!"

"Oh? What do you mean by that?"

"A happiness hunt is a hunt for happiness," the boy said. "By the way, miss, are you busy right now?"

Is he…asking me on a date? No, no, surely not.

"I guess you could say that I'm free, but you could also say that I'm busy."

"So you're free!"

……

"By the way, is there a village or town where people live nearby?" If I didn't find a place to stay, I'd be camping out in this meadow, and I can't say that was a very compelling option.

"If you're looking for a village, there's one over there." He pointed, and there was indeed a small village…or something village-esque. It seemed very isolated.

"Uh-huh."

"Actually, that's my village."

"Ah, so you're the village chief? Pleased to meet you. My name is Elaina. I'm a traveler."

"Oh, pleased to meet you. I'm Emil— Wait, no, that's not what I meant! I meant that's the village where I live." Emil puffed out his cheeks.

"I knew that. It was just a joke." I smiled.

Emil turned sulky and hugged his bottle instead of replying.

When I looked more closely at the bottle, I could just barely make out the shape of something wriggling inside it—a kind of floating white mist that moved like a living thing.

"What is that?" I pointed at the bottle.

He had probably wanted me to ask. With a proud snort, Emil gave me an answer. "This is the bottle where I'm collecting happiness! The instant a person or animal feels happiness, I transform it with a spell and gather it up in this bottle."

"Huh…"

Magic can move objects, transfigure things into flame or ice or…

anything else, really, and duplicate things right before your eyes. You can use it to fly on a broom, to make the wind blow, or to change yourself into a mouse. But gathering up happiness the moment it's felt means transforming emotion using a spell.

This might be interesting.

"Can I open it and look?"

"O-of course you can't!"

When I stretched out my hand, Emil squeezed the bottle even tighter in his arms and retreated a little. With a hostile look in his eye, he proclaimed, "I'm doing this for a girl I like, so I won't let you touch it!"

"Uh-huh."

"Um, are you mad?"

"No, I'm actually kind of impressed."

I recalled a book I had read a long time ago. It was the story of a husband who walked around outside, magically duplicating beautiful images the moment he saw them and taking them home to show to his sick wife who couldn't leave the house. *Now how did that story end, again?* It was a story from long, long ago, so I had completely forgotten.

"There's a girl you like?"

"Hmm? Yeah, she's a maid named Nino who works at my house. She always seems so gloomy, so I'm going to give her some happiness."

So that's why he's stuffing happiness into a bottle.

He held the bottle up high for me to see and stared at it lovingly. He looked quite content; if you really could transform the expression he was wearing right then, you could bottle up some really good happiness.

After that, we rode on our brooms and headed for the village. Emil was indeed a mage, but since he had mentioned magic spells earlier, there had been no need to ask. That said, I was very curious about what the boy had been doing in the middle of the meadow.

"I was testing to see whether I could take happiness from plants, too," Emil said, flying behind me.

"How did it go?" I asked.

"So-so. The spell let me transform something *like* emotion, but it was kind of hazy, and the color was cloudy. So I let it go."

"My, my."

Well, they are plants, after all. If you asked someone whether plants have distinct emotions, they would just look at you funny. Plus, if you knew the answer was yes, you might not be able to eat a salad ever again. Perhaps it's best to let some mysteries stay mysteries.

"Ah, there it is." He pointed to the village I could see just ahead.

It was a tiny village, small enough that you could probably walk the circumference of the pitiful perimeter fence in under an hour. There were only about ten houses sparsely populating the area, all built of wood. Some small fields and wells were interspersed among them, as if to fill in the gaps.

Oh, wow. "What a peaceful village."

"Isn't it?"

We got down off our brooms and passed between two trees that served as the gate for the village. Straight ahead of us on the road sat a house that was a large, splendid mansion in comparison to the others. By which I mean—well, it was about the same size as most normal houses in other countries.

"Is that the village chief's house?"

Pointing at the building, Emil nodded. "That's right. And it's my house, too."

"Oh?" Then it wasn't necessarily wrong to say this village was Emil's village.

"…You don't seem impressed, miss."

"Oh, should I have been more surprised? Wow, that's amazing, you must be really rich!"

"Um…I mean, that's not…" A shadow fell over Emil's expression.

"Anyway, Emil, when are you going to give that bottle to the girl?" I asked, and he lit up again. His emotional highs and lows were entertainingly extreme.

"Today! I'll give it to her after lunch. Oh yeah, you should join us! Nino's cooking is the best!"

"I'm happy you want to invite me, but I just ate."

"Okay, I'll have Nino make you a small plate! Are there any foods you can't eat? I'll ask her not to use them!"

It seemed like he wanted me to stay for lunch no matter what. *Well, I don't have any reason to refuse, do I?*

"No, I'm fine with anything, but I really did just have a meal, so please ask her for a small portion, okay?"

"Leave it to me! I'll get you some really yummy stuff!"

But you're not the one making the food. It's Nino.

○

And that's how I came to be a guest at the home of the village chief.

Despite the luxuriously large outward appearance of the house, the interior was totally average. The dining room that Emil showed me was decorated with old furniture, and the chief's household seemed to live a modest life just like the rest of the simple village. Actually, I was getting the impression that the estate was just a big plot of land they didn't know what to do with.

"Okay, have a seat." Emil pulled out a chair and gestured me toward it, and I sat.

"Thanks. By the way, where is that maid of yours?"

"I wonder… She'll probably be here soon."

"And the village chief?"

"He should get here soon, too."

"What's with that noncommittal attitude?"

After I spent some time conversing with Emil, I sensed someone coming up behind me. Not in a sixth-sense kind of way, though; I just heard the noise. Anyway, I turned around.

"…Ah."

There was a young girl. When our eyes met, she jumped in surprise and gave a small, frightened bow. It was really kind of pathetic.

Judging from her clothes, this is the maid in question. She wore an apron dress (the classic maid outfit) that was a little too big for her petite frame.

"How do you do? Might you be from the East?"

Her glossy black hair was pin straight, and her eyes were a deep, dark brown. She resembled a certain apprentice witch whom I had met in another country, also from the East. That apprentice's hair had been a little bit shorter, though.

"Ah? Uh, um…"

Maybe it was rude of me to suddenly ask where she came from. The bewildered girl glanced to Emil for help.

"Yes, she is. My father found Nino in an eastern country."

"I've heard they're having you work as a maid in this house?"

The girl called Nino gave a small nod. "Y-yes…the village chief treats me very kindly."

Her reply was mechanical, as if she was being compelled to read a script.

"Where is the village chief now?"

"Ah, um… He is in his study now, working…," she said, gripping the hem of her dress. "Um, did you have some business with him?"

"No, not really." I shook my head.

I'm probably going to meet him when it's time to eat anyway, so there's no need to press.

When that little exchange was over, Nino lowered her gaze as if to avoid making eye contact. She didn't seem particularly good at talking to people.

But the boy who loved her didn't care at all as he bounded over to her and leaned down to see her eyes. "Hey, hey, Nino, what's for lunch today?" I couldn't see his expression because his back was to me, but I'm sure it was a broad smile.

"Ah, t-today is…grilled fish, on request from the village chief."

"Yay! Say, if it's all right, could I get you to make some for that girl, too?" Emil pointed at me. Nino looked at me for a moment and nodded slightly.

"See, miss?"

"I appreciate it. Thank you, but I'm not very hungry, so please make mine a small portion."

"…Y-yes, miss." As Emil had said, Nino certainly was gloomy. If someone walked in just then and saw her face, they might assume the two of us were bullying her.

"Oh yeah! Hey, Nino, after we eat lunch today, I have a present for you."

"Ah, f-for me…?"

"Yep. Hope you're excited!"

"N-no…that's all right. I-if you give something to a servant like me…the village chief will be angry…" Even beyond the humble phrasing, it was a particularly servile thing to say.

"It's fine, it's fine. I'll explain it all to Father."

"Oh, but…"

Impatient, Emil played his trump card against the meek girl. "Well then, it's an order from me. How about that?"

"……"

His feelings must have gotten through to her; after all, he was very direct, maybe overly so. Nino nodded slowly. "If it's an order…," she said, then smiled faintly.

He smiled back at her.

I was quite bored for the next little while.

Emil diligently went to assist Nino, leaving the guest (me) all alone in the dining room. I had also headed to the kitchen to lend a hand, but Emil turned me away with a dazzling smile. "You go sit down, miss! The two of us will do the cooking!"

There was no one to talk to and nothing to do but wait for the time to pass, extremely unproductively. *I can't sit still. I want to read a book or something. But I don't carry books around...*

I ended up passing the time doing nothing but sitting in my chair.

I had been waiting several minutes when a plump man sat down across from me.

"Ah, a rare guest."

He wasn't especially old or young, possibly late thirties or early forties. Maybe. I guess?

"Good afternoon. Would you happen to be the village chief?" I asked, convinced that he must be.

"Indeed." See?

"I am Elaina, a friend of your son's. I'm a traveler. Nice to meet you."

"A pleasure to make your acquaintance. I am Emil's father."

I know that. And now he had made his appearance with perfect timing. Exactly when I was in need of something to do.

"Mr. Village Chief, how long have you been in charge around here?"

"Since the very beginning."

"Is that so?"

"Mm."

"It's a lovely village."

"Mm."

"Do you have any local culinary specialties that you're known for?"

"No."

"Not at all?"

"Mm."

"...Is that so?"

I feel like I continued this futile attempt at conversation with the chief in bits and pieces, but I have absolutely no recollection of what we discussed.

To put it bluntly, I learned nothing.

After a little while, Nino and Emil brought in the food. As the two of them prepared the table, my faint feelings of hunger were accompanied by an indescribable unease.

"......"

I could've sworn I only asked them for a small portion.

○

"Huh? We did make it small!" Emil replied, staring at me in puzzlement. "See, the fish is small, and we gave you a little less salad."

Well, now that you mention it, I can tell you gave me a little less, but I would have been fine with less than half of what you prepared.

"Um...p-perhaps it really is too much...? If you can't finish it, please feel free to leave some behind..."

"......"

I was silenced before I could say anything.

Standing next to Nino, Emil was glaring at me. And his eyes said, "*Don't you dare leave any behind.*"

I ate it. I cleaned my plate, in fact. It truly was a very delicious meal, but I only tasted the first few bites. After that, it became a chore of cramming the remaining amount into my stomach. What a waste.

"Thanks for the meal! That was really delicious, Nino."

"Th-thank you...very much." Nino gave an embarrassed little bow. "I'll clean up the dishes..." She stood up and gathered the plates and glasses. Emil lent a hand, as if it was a matter of course.

In that case, I'll help, too. I started to stand up, but again Emil turned to me with a smile and said, "Oh, you're fine, miss."

As the two of them headed for the kitchen, I posed a question to the village chief. "Where did you meet Miss Nino?"

After draining the rest of the water in his glass, the village chief answered me. "I bought her in the Orient," he said, as if it were the most ordinary thing in the world.

Bought. *In other words...* "She's a slave?"

"Mm. I got her several years ago. My wife left us, and for a while, I couldn't handle all the housework."

"……"

There was plenty that I wanted to say, but I refrained. Silently, I prompted him to continue.

"Back in those days, I traveled to the East from time to time for work, and that's where I found her. The price was a little higher than I would have preferred, but she was adequate at housework, and more importantly, she had a nice face and looked like she would grow up to be a beautiful woman. I bought her without a second thought, and it was a good decision. She's made a fine maid."

The chief let out a vulgar laugh.

"Does Emil know?"

"I think I told him, but he doesn't seem to mind much that his play-mate is a slave."

Emil had said the village chief had "found" Nino, so he might not have realized she was a slave.

But even if Nino had been bought, I had a feeling that Emil wouldn't change his behavior toward her at all. He seemed to treat everyone the same.

Nino returned quietly from the kitchen the moment our conversation broke off, glanced at our glasses to make sure they were empty, and then cleared them one by one from the table. She kept her head down the whole time. I think she had overheard our conversation.

"Hey, Nino, where should I put this big plate, again?"

"Eek…!"

There was an ear-splitting crash.

Emil had suddenly come out of the kitchen, and Nino had collided with him on her way back in, dropping the glasses in her hands. Shards of all sizes were scattered around their feet.

"What the hell are you doing?!" the chief roared from across the table. He stood up in a rage and grabbed the stupefied Nino by the lapels of her apron. "Clean this up immediately, you worthless girl!

How long will I have to wait before you can complete all of your tasks perfectly?!"

"I-I'm sorry, I'm sorry, I'm sorry, I'm sorry…"

"Stop it, Father! That was my fault, wasn't it?! Don't just blame Nino—"

"Shut your mouth, boy!" Emil shuddered and hung his head.

Apparently deciding he had yelled enough, the chief let go of Nino and jerked his chin toward the glass. "Clean that up."

With tears welling in her eyes, Nino nodded and bowed over and over to the two of them and to me. "I'm sorry, I'm sorry, I'm sorry…," she repeated, as if the words were a spell to protect her.

This is extremely unpleasant. Really, this is so uncomfortable.

I pushed back my chair, crouched over the wreckage of the glasses, and pulled out my wand. "This isn't bad at all. As long as you have all the pieces, you don't need to clean it up."

I used a convenient time-reversing spell designed to fix wounds and repair things. A white mist-like substance brushed the transparent shards. As time reversed, the pieces gathered together, then returned to their original form.

I handed the restored glasses to Nino. "Next time, be careful not to drop them, okay?"

I could tell she had no idea what had just happened.

"Oh, thank you. You fixed the glasses even after witnessing that disgrace," the village chief interjected from beside me in a calm voice. "Hey, you thank her, too."

Wait, you shouldn't force people to say thank you.

"…I'm sorry." What's more, Nino had missed the point and said the wrong thing. She was bowing deeply.

"Don't apologize, say thank you, Nino," I said.

Nino raised her head and choked out the words in a tearful voice. "Thank you…very much."

○

"I can do spells like that, too, you know."

After the village chief had shut himself in his study and Nino had gone back to washing dishes, Emil grew sullen.

You don't have to put on a brave front.

"Oh no, I'm sorry. In that case, you didn't need my help at all."

"No, I did, because I couldn't do anything. Thank you, miss."

"Don't mention it."

"But just so you know, I *can* do that."

"……"

It must be embarrassing to have your weakness exposed in front of the girl you like.

"You don't really have anything to worry about." I clapped a hand on his shoulder. "Anyway, right now, Nino must be very upset. Isn't this your best chance to give her your present?"

"Miss, you're a genius…"

"Oh-ho, do go on."

His hopes rekindled, Emil's mood improved immediately. *He's such a simple child. It's adorable, really.*

Hiding the bottle behind his back, Emil waited for Nino to finish her work.

"…Ah." Nino trudged out of the kitchen and cringed in surprise when Emil suddenly appeared before her, like a small animal. Maybe she remembered running into him earlier.

Emil took a step toward her. "Nino, I told you that I had a present for you after lunch, didn't I?"

"…Y-yes," Nino answered hesitantly.

"Here. This is your present."

Emil held the bottle out to her. Nino stared, nonplussed, at the squirming white haze inside. She clearly had no idea what this was.

"This here is a bottle that I've filled with happiness." Emil put his hand on the cap. "Inside it's full of happiness. I went all over collecting it from people."

"…People's happiness?"

Nino tilted her head in confusion, and Emil grinned.

"You can only see it once, so watch closely, okay?"

With a satisfying *shunk*, he uncapped the bottle. Now that it was free, the white mist flew out of the bottle, up to the ceiling. When the ceiling was completely covered with white clouds, small particles began slowly swirling around in the mist.

Like shards of glass, the particles sparkled with reflected light to create a fantastic display. The shining particles were the fragments of happiness Emil had collected, projecting the scenes that had inspired them.

Joy at the birth of a child. The contentment of viewing a picturesque landscape. The subtle delight of finding a pretty flower. The satisfaction of overcoming a hardship. The quiet pleasure of sprawling out in the sunlight to read a book on a day off and dozing without a care.

"The outside world is full of so much happiness, you see." Emil took Nino's hand. "So don't be so sad all the time. I'll be here to make you happy, too."

As for Nino, she watched the shining lights in amazement, and before long she was silently weeping. She held a hand over her mouth to stifle the sound as the tears trickled down her cheeks.

Emil smiled, a little confused, and gently embraced her.

The tears flowing down her face glittered just like the fragments of happiness.

○

"You could stay a little bit longer."

We were at the two trees that stood in place of a gate. Emil had come to the edge of the village to see me off, and he was pouting like an abandoned puppy. Next to him stood the maid, Nino. She had never been very expressive, so I couldn't tell whether she was saddened by my departure.

I shook my head. "Sorry, but I can't take it too easy," I said, taking out my broom.

"...Come see us again then, okay? Nino and I will cook for you again, and it'll be even better next time. Okay?"

"Y-yes...we'll be waiting." Nino gave a little bow.

I got on my broom and rose into the air. "Okay. I'll come again. Someday—definitely."

When my travels are at an end, perhaps.

The two of them waved at me as I receded—Emil waving both arms around wildly, and Nino waving calmly and delicately.

"......?"

I accidentally made eye contact with Nino.

Her eyes were like deep darkness, and I mean more than just the color. They were longing, desperate, as if she were in a state of unimaginable despair. As if she were already dead. It was nothing like when we'd first met in the village chief's mansion.

...I wonder why.

I was within sight of the next road when I remembered the ending of that book I read long ago.

The story of a husband who walked around outside, magically capturing beautiful vistas the moment he saw them, and taking them home to show his sick wife, who couldn't leave the house.

I wonder how I forgot about it until just now. It left such an awful aftertaste.

The story ended when the wife, who yearned to see the scenery for herself, forced her weakened body to move and died even sooner than she was supposed to. It was a fable, and the moral was "The things we think we do for the sake of others are not always what's best for them."

What was Nino thinking after she saw the contents of that bottle, I wonder? What decision would she have reached? She couldn't possibly—

"........."

No, no way. She wouldn't.

When I looked back, the wind was running through the broad meadow of brilliant green. The wildflowers shone in the sunlight, like the surface of still water swaying in the wind.

It really was a beautiful place. But I had no reason to ever return.

If I did, I would just end up feeling sad.

CHAPTER 7

Before the Match Begins

I arrived at a certain country in the morning. I had found it by coincidence while flying over the plains on my broom, so I had absolutely no idea what kind of place it was.

In villages too small for a gate, an immigration inspection is unnecessary, but whenever you enter a country that has some territory to it, the gate guards always have questions for you. That said, unless something unusual is going on, they always ask the same ones.

"Name?"

"Elaina."

"Country of origin?"

"The Peaceful Country of Robetta."

"Reason for entry?"

"Sightseeing."

"Length of stay?"

"Probably three days."

Usually the questions end there, you pay the entry fee if there is one, and the guard should say, "Welcome, and take care" as he steps back to let you in…

"For breakfast, do you take bread or rice?"

…However, the questions continued. And with a very odd question at that.

"…What?" I frowned and asked him in return.

Without so much as a twitch, the guard repeated himself. "With breakfast, do you eat bread? Or do you eat rice? This information is required upon entry, so please answer honestly."

There must be some kind of dispute going on in their culinary scene. Well, he says it's required information, so I should answer honestly. Though I think the question is a little out of place in an official procedure.

"I don't have a preference. I'm a traveler, so I intend to adapt to the tastes of the places that I visit."

I mean, I can't say "I only eat bread!" in a country where they always eat rice. And the opposite is also true, of course. I'll maintain a neutral stance.

"Hmm... How unusual," said the guard, stroking his beard before continuing. "I see. In that case, I'll put you down for both." Then he stepped back and said, "Please take care, Madam Witch."

After bowing to the guard, I passed through the gate.

○

I immediately understood the reason behind the strange question.

It looked like two different cultures met here.

When I came out of the gate, there was a large canal right in front of me. With the canal as the dividing line, the houses to the right were all built in the Eastern style, while the houses to the left were all built in the Western style.

Immediately in front of the gate, there were two roads. The sign to the right said EAST TOWN: RICE EATERS THIS WAY! while the other said WEST TOWN: BREAD EATERS THIS WAY!

It looks like the country is divided into two factions: rice and bread.

"...Hmm." I was stuck. I really didn't care either way.

But come to think of it, this might be my first time walking through an Eastern-style town. I'm always traveling through Western-style towns. All right then, it's decided.

I veered right.

The road was lined with neatly placed square stones, and dignified wooden houses formed neat rows. I could see the royal palace ahead and surmised that it was placed at the center of the divide, like the canal.

About halfway down the road to the palace, there was a bridge. The brand-new structure was somewhat at odds with the historical townscape. I could see a small boat passing through the middle of the circle formed by the bridge and its reflection on the water.

"……?"

I cocked my head in confusion at the strange figures on the boat.

There was a man sitting on the handrail eating breakfast. He was clad in Eastern clothes, so clearly, he was a resident of East Town. But even when I doubled-checked, he was definitely holding a piece of bread. *A rice person is eating bread.*

Next to the man, a woman was stuffing her cheeks with a delicious-looking rice ball. *She appears to be a member of the rice faction, but she's wearing a Western-style dress.*

I was intrigued. It was a very strange scene.

"Um, excuse me?" I called out to the two of them.

After sharing a glance with the woman, the man answered me. "Yes, what is it?"

You've got bread in your hand, but you're wearing Eastern clothes. That's odd.

I asked a simple, clear question. "What kind of country is this anyway?"

"What kind of country? Hmm." The man crossed his arms, and then left the answering up to the woman next to him. "How would you answer that?"

"A great country."

"Yeah! It *is* a great country. Miss Traveler, you're here in a great country."

That's not what I meant to ask. I meant more like, well…

"The townscape is great, but you're even better."

"Nooo, *you* are."

"Oh-ho-ho."

"Ah-ha-ha."

......

It seems I'm just a third wheel here. I should probably leave now.

Plus, I get the sense that asking these two isn't going to get me the information I want, so it's not like I'm cutting our conversation short, is it? No, I mean it.

At any rate, I thanked them and left.

I walked around both the Eastern and Western parts of town for as long as time would permit in the hopes of finding some information.

However, the longer I walked, the stranger it got. I hadn't been able to tell because there were so few people out in the morning, but in the afternoon when the streets were full, there were so many people crossing the bridge that it was like there was no clear division at all.

Even stranger, despite their own signs reading WE CANNOT SELL TO MEMBERS OF THE RICE FACTION, the bread stalls were brazenly handing over their goods to people in Eastern clothing.

It wasn't only the stalls; every store in town seemed to have a regulation in place, from the dry goods store to the greengrocer to any number of others. They all had signs on display prohibiting service to customers who came from the opposite side of town. However, everyone ignored them. The signs had absolutely no purpose.

Returning to East Town from West Town, I parted the curtain of a dumpling shop.

"Welcome. What will you have?"

I sat down in a chair, and a young woman dressed in Eastern clothes crouched before me. I pointed to the sign outside that said WE CANNOT SELL TO MEMBERS OF THE BREAD FACTION, and said, "I'm a bread eater."

"Is that a joke?" The waitress covered her mouth politely with one hand and giggled.

"A joke?"

She smiled up at me and said, "No one pays any attention to those decorations!"

Of course. I can see that just by observing the state of the town. But what's the point of the signs, then?

"Your order?"

"Oh, I'll have three sweet-soy-glazed rice dumplings, please."

"Coming right up."

○

Still feeling uneasy, I hunted for an inn on the Western side of town.

There are lodgings on the Eastern side, too, but I can't stay over there. I can't sleep unless I'm in a proper bed. Or maybe I just have a harder time adjusting to Eastern-style rooms. I'm not the biggest fan of walking barefoot on straw mats.

I walked around and around the town, then went into the cheapest-looking inn. It had a sign out front that read WE DECLINE THE PATRONAGE OF MEMBERS OF THE RICE FACTION.

Well, let's just ignore that.

"Evenin'." When I entered, the indifferent-looking innkeeper was resting his chin in his hands over at the counter.

"One night's stay, please," I said, taking out a silver coin.

"Thank ya. Go on and fill out the form."

"Sure."

I was already used to these forms. I finished filling it out with a series of quick pen strokes. As I handed the completed form over to the innkeeper, I asked him, "If you don't mind, could I ask you to tell me a bit about this place?"

"…Haven't seen ya 'round here before, ma'am. You a traveler?"

"Yes. And this land is so strange I can hardly wrap my brain around it."

The innkeeper was quiet for a moment, then said, "Whaddaya wanna know?"

Oh, he gets it. As one would expect from a person who regularly does business with travelers.

"All right, tell me the reason why West Town and East Town are so different from each other."

The innkeeper finally gave me the information I had been craving.

"Back in the day, this land was two neighboring countries that straddled the canal. The country on the east side had inherited an Eastern culture, and the country on the west side a Western one. Each country had its own king. The two kings got along well, and there was a great relationship between the countries—well, it wasn't all that different from how it is now."

"Mm-hmm." *Simple enough.*

"One day, the two kings got to talkin'. They said, 'Why not make the two countries into one?' No one had any gripes about it since West and East both wanted the same thing. Actually, it felt like the decision was long overdue."

"Was that when the bridges between the two towns were built?"

The innkeeper nodded. "Yep. The kings built those to commemorate the merger."

"I see." *That must be why they're so new and out of place.*

"A while after that, the two kings each had a child. The king on the Western side had a daughter, and the king on the Eastern side had a son. The kids got along just like their fathers, and eventually got married. They built a palace right off the canal—in the exact middle of the united country—and started living there. Now the two of them have become a symbol of our land. And that's about all I know," the innkeeper said, placing the key for my room on the counter.

I took it and said, "Thank you very much. By the way, mister, can I ask you one more thing?"

"What's that?"

I told him about the strange question I had been asked when I entered the country, and about the weird signs by the gate and in front of the stores, and about the couple I had met on the bridge. "At first, I thought the country was divided internally, but looking around me, it seems like people don't pay any attention to the signs at all. They cross the bridges and intermingle just fine. So what's the point of having the signboards at all?"

The innkeeper listened quietly as I spoke and nodded when I was finished. "Mm. Those signs are in preparation for the big match."

He said it so matter-of-factly, I wondered if I'd misheard. "Big match? What on earth does that mean?"

"I hear they want to unify the country under either Eastern or Western culture. Well, that's why the gate guards are asking strange questions anyway, and it's the reason for the signs."

Perhaps after this country was merged under the good auspices of the kings of the previous generation, there's a movement to split them apart again.

But why?

"Those two don't know the meaning of the word *compromise*," the innkeeper said with a laugh.

Incidentally, he charged me an "information fee" after the fact.

O

After I had spent several days there, I began getting ready to set off again. This blend of Western and Eastern cultures was of course quite fascinating, but if I may be blunt, that was the only thing it had going for it.

I felt like I had seen enough.

Ultimately, I was leaving without understanding an essential part of the place, but oh well...right? I didn't care enough to really go digging for answers. Though I would listen if anyone cared to explain why the signboards were up.

Well, that's all right. Trying to convince myself that I didn't care, I passed through the gate—

"Ah, wait a minute, please, Miss Witch."

—and was stopped. The guard was holding his spear out in front of him, blocking my path.

"…Um, what is it?" I'm sure I looked very confused.

"If you can, would you please give us a little more of your time?"

"…? Why would I do that?"

Depending on the time and the situation and the reason, I wasn't opposed to hearing what he had to say. *If it's something silly, I'm going to say no and leave, though.*

"You've been summoned by the lord and lady."

"……Huh?"

Well, it appears the reason isn't silly at all.

We proceeded all the way down the canal, where I was shown to the castle watching over both cultures. They walked me through the perplexing interior of the keep, a blend of Eastern and Western styles, and finally we arrived at an enormous reception hall.

The hall looked like a Western-style room and an Eastern-style room had been cut in two, and one half of each had been stuck together.

It doesn't go together at all…

I heard someone closing the door behind me as I stepped into the room, and I could see two thrones a little farther ahead. The man and woman seated there appeared to be in the middle of an argument. They didn't seem to notice me there at all.

"I'm telling you, the match ought to be a game of *shogi*! There's no other way!"

"That's because you're better at *shogi*! How many times do I have to tell you we ought to play chess!"

"And how many times do I have to tell *you*, you're better at chess!"

"Grrr…"

"Rrrr…"

The volatile atmosphere seemed like it might erupt into violence at any minute as the two of them glared at each other from their thrones.

I cleared my throat to let them know that I was there. Not the most polite thing to do in the presence of royalty, but it *was* effective in getting them to notice me.

"Huh? You must be…"

"The traveler, aren't you? My, my…"

I bowed. "I was told that Your Highnesses had some business with me, so I came as soon as I was called. How can I be of service?"

"Mm. The truth is—"

The king opened his mouth to speak, but the queen cut him off.

"I'll tell the witch, so you can stop there."

"What the—? I'll explain…"

"No, I will."

Will someone hurry up and tell me what's going on? I don't care who it is… Hello…?

Eventually, after arguing in circles, the king took the lead and told me everything.

"The fact is: This land is on the brink of war. As you can see, this woman and I are not getting along. We agreed to settle things with a contest, but now we can't decide what the contest should be. I've heard you are a neutral party, not associated with either faction, so we want you to decide how we proceed."

"…You can't decide on the contest?" *No, before that…* "First of all, would you begin by telling me why you want to hold this contest in the first place?"

The king raised his voice, "Because *she* insulted the people of the Western side! She said, 'People who don't eat rice for breakfast aren't human'!"

Without a moment's delay, the queen interrupted him with an objection. "No, it's because *you* said, 'People who don't eat bread for breakfast are lower than dogs'!"

"Okay, enough. Both of you be quiet a moment, please."

"……" "……"

This was getting exasperating, so I shut them up and took control of the situation myself. I turned the conversation back to the king. "Your Highness, when I entered this land, the first thing I saw was a strange signboard. It was a perplexing sign, meant to divide the rice faction and the bread faction, but tell me—exactly what purpose does that serve?"

"It makes it easier to see which side has more people."

"We put them in place so that we could tell which one was more influential."

Why is the queen answering, too…? Well, whatever. Calling her out on it would be too much trouble.

"And what has the result been?" I asked.

The king answered, "There are more people on the Western side."

"There are more people of influence on the Eastern side," the queen added.

"That's why I said we should decide based on the larger number of people."

"No. We should decide a winner based on financial clout. Obviously."

"You don't understand a thing, and you never have."

"I could say the same about you."

"……"

"……"

As the two of them glared at each other again, I suddenly remembered something. What had they been shouting about when I first entered the reception hall? It was chess and *shogi*, wasn't it?

If the argument is over whether to decide through majority rule or through financial leverage, then why were they talking about board games?

Without even waiting for my response, the two of them obstinately resumed their argument. "So we can't decide after all. In that case, I want to choose the method for determining the method for determining the method for determining the method for determining the method for determining the method for determining the method for determining the method for determining the method of holding the match with a game of chess."

"No. *Shogi.*"

"......"

"You don't understand. If we play *shogi*, you're better at it!"

"You don't understand, you always win at chess!"

"......"

I felt like I had just gotten a peek behind the curtain. Just to be sure, I asked the king and queen, "By the way, when did this quarrel begin?"

The two of them turned to me and answered simultaneously, "Two years ago."

"Ah, I see. Well then, I think you should probably let it go, because you're never going to solve this," I said, and left the palace. The two of them kept on yelling and made no attempt to stop me.

O

Now I understood why the residents of each town totally ignored the signboards. It had been two years since the king and queen had said they were going to hold a contest and unify under one culture or the other. Time had just passed by without anything happening, and none of the citizens probably cared about a bunch of signboards erected for the sake of a quarrel.

The signs had already become nothing more than decorations.

Looking at it a different way, it was a sign that the authority of the crown had become meaningless. Right now, no one in the whole land was actually paying attention to what the royals said.

"Ah, Madam Witch. How did you like our country?"

The guard came out to greet me as I returned to the gate from the palace. I passed right by him, and only turned around after I had set foot in the outside world.

Gazing at the curious collision of cultures, I said, "It's a nice, peaceful place." *Though I can't speak for its future.*

Maybe the king and queen would realize they had been wasting their time and turn their attention back to ruling. Maybe they would keep dragging it out, and the whole place would get stranger and stranger. Or maybe everything would stay as it was.

Whatever ended up happening, it was no concern of mine.

"That's right; it is a nice place, isn't it?"

The gate guard nodded with satisfaction.

CHAPTER 8

On the Road: The Tale of Two Men Who Fought Over a Girl

Rainfall sent the fragrance of flowers wafting through the forest. The grass and trees glittered in the sunlight filtering down through the canopy. A lovely girl flew by, riding a broom down the sole path to her destination.

Upon her breast was a star-shaped brooch. From her pointy hat, which she diligently kept in place with one hand as she flew, to the black robe covering her body, she looked every bit a witch. Just who could she be?

That's right. She's me.

I was flying along on my broom, headed for the country closest to the one I had left a few days ago—the one divided between Eastern and Western cultures. From what I had heard, the country ahead was very, very plain. Just an ordinary place full of people who were ever so slightly more muscular than average. Exactly *what* is normal about that is another question.

Well, if they're anything like a certain individual I met some time ago whose muscles have replaced his brain, I suppose they might live quite happily, but…I'll probably only spend one day there and then leave.

Such thoughts wandered through my mind as I gazed at the scenery speeding past.

To put it bluntly, I had nothing to do. That's why my ears perked up when I heard some distant noise in the still forest.

"All right, let's go over the rules one more time. The two of us are going to make one lap around the forest path, and first person back to this spot gets to be her boyfriend. Is that right?"

"Y-yeah. No problems here."

"...No cheating, right?"

"N-naturally. I w-would never do something like that."

"...I wonder..."

One man had a lively, energetic voice, while the other sounded heavy and muffled. *Sounds like they're having a race. Sounds interesting*, I thought, when there came another voice.

"Huh? You mean I have to wait here all by myself? That sounds boooring!"

The sugary-sweet voice of a young woman echoed clearly through the air, catching me by surprise. My focus shifted from my own thoughts back to the outside world, and I was surprised again when I found myself making eye contact with her.

"Well, today's my lucky day!" mumbled the cute girl with black hair.

...Ugh.

O

It felt wrong to fly on past after making eye contact, so I slowed down. Unfortunately, that was my first mistake. As I pulled up closer to the black-haired girl, she grabbed me and pulled me down off my broom.

"Kyah! So cute! Oh, that brooch is something only witches have, right? Wow! That means you're a witch, right?"

"Um, yes..."

"Amazing! You're so cute but you're a witch, too?! That's so cool!"

"Uh, thanks..."

"So you can do magic, right? I mean, you were just flying on a broom! Wow!"

"Sure, yeah..."

"By the way, do you have a moment, like, right now?"

"No, um…"

"Yippee! Now I have somebody to wait with!"

"Um…" *Just a second! Listen to what I'm saying!*

The girl practically dragged me over to where two guys were standing, all the while calling me "cute" and wowing over and over again. The two guys looked me up and down.

"You're gonna wait with a witch, huh? Well, I guess we won't have to worry about you getting attacked by a bear or something. Good, good," said the handsome man.

"Y-yeah. It's a relief. Whew," the plump man said, breathing heavily.

……

I whispered to the girl standing next to me, "Just what is going on here, exactly?"

"What do you mean?" she asked, confused. "I'm sorry, I didn't explain yet, did I? You see, these two are fighting over me."

No, I got that much. I could hear you when I was flying in. That's not what I'm asking.

"These two are fighting over you, are they?" I spoke in a very low voice so that the two men couldn't hear me.

"Yes…?" I could hear her unspoken question in her tone: *"Is that strange?"*

Feeling a sudden and very complicated swirl of emotions, I took a second look at the two men. The well-spoken man gave a broad smile so bright, even his teeth sparkled. And standing next to this immaculate man, the plump man was soaked with sweat. He looked smelly. A real piece of work.

Despite the obvious, enormous gulf between their outward appearances, the girl was having them compete against each other. *Is she an idiot? I'm not sure what she's thinking. But maybe the plump man has some sort of hidden talent. Or maybe the eloquent one has a really bad personality?*

……

Alas, my interest was piqued. "I see, I see. Well then, I'll assume responsibility for protecting her."

Whatever was going on, I was a part of it now.

"Ready, go!"

When I clapped my hands, the two of them took off running at the same time.

"Raaah! Her heart is mine!" Mr. Perfect started out enthusiastically.

"Ngh, phew...hah, hah." Mr. Porky was exhausted the moment they started running.

Huh? How strange. I expected Mr. Porky to be unleashing his awesome hidden power right about now.

After the two had completely disappeared, I turned to question the girl. "Why are you having them compete?"

"Hmm?" she asked in a muffled voice as she took a carefree drink of water. She pointed to the water bottle. "Who do you think got this water for me?"

"Didn't you get it yourself?"

She shook her head. "Fatty got this for me. He doesn't take care of his appearance, but he's attentive to the little things, you see."

"Fatty?" *She must mean Mr. Porky. That's a very...direct nickname. It's not incorrect, though.*

"Oh, by the way, there's one for you, too."

"...Why is there one for me?" I was confused. *But I just happened to come by.*

"He slipped it to me just before the race started. It seems he brought a spare, so I'll give it to you." She pushed the bottle into my hands.

I'm not particularly thirsty, but I'll take it anyway. The water inside the bottle sparkled, reflecting the sunlight. *But now I understand. He certainly is attentive. Who would have thought he'd have a water bottle for me, too?*

"So you've been charmed by the heart and soul of the plump guy, and the appearance and manners of the well-spoken guy, is that it? What a nice problem to have." *I'm not jealous, though.*

The girl laughed dryly. "I don't really like Fatty at all, though, you know?" She quickly brushed aside my assumptions.

...*Huh?* "What are you talking about?"

I was sure she was pitting them against each other because she couldn't decide.

"*Fwah.*" The girl finished drinking all of the water in her bottle, then answered me gleefully. "I just messed around with Fatty because I had nothing better to do."

"......"

"But he's useless. Does he think this tiny bottle of water would be enough? I'm still thirsty." She threw the empty bottle into the forest.

Sure, I hadn't been exactly kind to the big man in my own internal monologue, and I wasn't particularly proud of that, but in that very moment, a single wish filled my heart. I sent a plea out to the universe.

Let this woman receive divine punishment.

○

And boy, did it ever.

It happened several minutes after the girl had thrown the empty bottle into the forest. I noticed her suddenly yawning dramatically, and then she just kept leaning, until she fell over backward with a *thud*.

Thankfully the underbrush made a nice cushion, so she didn't hit her head too hard.

I chided her inwardly, then started panicking and wondering if she was dead because she had fallen over so suddenly. But as I got closer, I could hear the distinct sound of snoring.

And that was how I found myself relaxing with this girl's head in my lap in the shade of the trees.

"Wheeh...muscles, so many muscles..."

This girl's attitude is awful, and the way she sleeps is just as awful. What visions of hell must she be seeing for there to be nothing but muscles?

I wasted several minutes staring at her drool-covered face and listening to her terrible sleep talk. Then a single silhouette appeared in the distance. *Who could that be? Well, there's no need to wonder, the first one to return is obviously going to be…*

"……Ah." I blinked a few times and looked back at the figure running toward me. But no matter how many times I checked, the person approaching us was *him*.

It was Mr. Porky.

It was Fatty.

…*How?*

Huffing and puffing, covered in sweat and grease, he finally reached us with a triumphant grin. "Heh, hah… I did it, I w-won… heh…"

Ah, I was foolish to feel sympathy for him earlier. As he looked around and confirmed that Mr. Perfect had not yet returned, his expression was extremely revolting.

The phrase *physically impossible* crossed my mind. *Yeah, this is actually physically impossible.*

But where was Mr. Perfect? My gaze followed Mr. Porky's dripping sweat and led me to the answer as I saw a figure approaching with tremendous speed.

It was Mr. Perfect.

When he saw Mr. Porky sneering, Mr. Perfect burst into tears. If it had just been him alone, or if there had been a beautiful girl waiting for him at the destination, the sight of such a softhearted man running in tears might have made a nice picture, but since the person in front of him was a pudgy man, the scene was just extremely surreal.

The man reached the finish line and immediately began his laments.

"D-dammit… Why, why…?! Why did I take a nap in the middle of the race?!"

A nap? Are you stupid?

The fairy tale of the slowpoke tortoise and the quick-footed hare suddenly crossed my mind. As I recalled, the way that story ended was that the careless hare took a nap, and the tortoise who kept giving their all won at the end. It was a stirring story that left the reader frustrated and cursing the tortoise.

Was this a repeat of that fable?

"Did you get careless?"

Wiping away the sheen of sweat and tears covering his face, Mr. Perfect answered, "No... I got sleepy in the middle of the race and passed out, and when I came to, I was sleeping just over there." He slumped his shoulders.

...Hmm. Is this what I think it is? I wondered.

Mr. Perfect must have been thinking the same thing. He whipped a finger out to point at Mr. Porky and shouted, "You put drugs in that water to make me sleepy, didn't you?!"

Yep, called it. In fact, there was one more person who had drunk the water he provided, and she was fast asleep in my lap.

Mr. Porky shrugged his shoulders at Mr. Perfect in a dramatic display of contempt.

"Heh, hah... Do you have any proof?" For some reason, it was incredibly irritating to me that he had suddenly decided to become talkative after the race was over.

But it looks like he dug his own grave. Taking care not to wake her up, I slowly lowered the sleeping girl's head from my lap and stood up.

"If you want proof, here it is—" Just as the words left my mouth and I shoved the bottle out at him, I realized it was already empty. Of course, there was no proof there.

I had had a bad feeling about it, so I had dumped out the contents.

What a mistake.

As I stood there awkwardly, Mr. Porky's mood seemed to improve even further. "See?! You don't have any proof anywhere! All right, she's mine! Hee-hee!"

"...Ugh."

"...Ugh."

Unfortunately, there was no way to prove he had done something wrong— *Wait, no. Wasn't there one more thing?*

I put the bottle down and picked up the sleeping girl. "Wait a minute. Here's the proof."

"Hee… Be sensible. Surely she just got tired and took a little nap."

"No, she went to sleep after drinking the water you gave her."

"Where's your proof? Is that all you have to say? I'm waiting."

"……"

Ooh, he makes me mad…!

Now, the girl was a terrible person for messing around with Mr. Porky, to be sure, but he had managed to surpass her. He was genuinely evil. *I should blast him away with magic.*

…Oh, I know just the thing.

I might have lost my cool, but Mr. Porky was maddening, and plus, he had started it.

I was furious.

I took out my wand—

"Wait right there."

There was a voice from above—one I may or may not have heard before.

When I looked up, the giant from the other day was standing there imposingly. Flanking him were two identical men who differed only in the color of their clothing.

Oh? What have we here?

This time (and this time only) I really felt like they were my saviors.

○

"Hello again." I bowed quickly to the three who had descended on us, and the big guy flexed his facial muscles… By which I mean he smiled.

"It's been a while, Madam Witch."

"Indeed it has, Muscleman."

It was the incredibly brawny man I had met several days earlier. I didn't know his real name, but I don't think he really minded. He was a strange person whose heart leaped with excitement at the sound of the very word *muscle*.

He puffed out his chest. "Mm, that's right. I *am* a muscular man."

Seems his skull is still full of muscle, too.

"It's nice to see you two again as well." I also bowed to the two men standing on either side of Muscleman.

"Good to see you."

"Yeah, hello again."

It seemed the two of them had gained more muscle mass. They had tried to trick me, but seeing their sinewy new physiques, I felt a little sorry for them.

"Brother, hasn't your skin tanned a bit?"

"I could say the same to you."

"Ha-ha-ha."

"Ha-ha-ha."

Eh, scratch that.

They seemed to be living the workout life. I ignored the two of them as they launched into some trivial conversation and quietly explained the details of the situation to Muscleman.

Muscleman was livid. "Oh-ho, so the smelly fat one is at fault, is he? Hmm?"

"N-no way! I d-d-didn't do anything! I won fair and square!"

"Don't lie." Muscleman grabbed him by the collar.

"Reeee!" Mr. Porky let out a groan that was more like a squeal. "I-I'm not lying!"

"Well, I suppose I'll just have to question you until I believe your story."

"S-stop it! You're being unfair! You just think that an ugly guy like me can't get a girlfriend, and you're laughing at me in your heads! But I fought hard, and I won! That's the truth! Why can't you just believe me?!" Flecks of spittle flew from his mouth as he spoke.

That seemed to upset Muscleman even more, and trust me, I noticed.

At this rate, the cowardly Mr. Porky was asking for a public execution.

Well, that's fine with me.

"......Mm." I was watching absentmindedly as Muscleman hoisted Mr. Porky into the air when I heard a voice behind me. Maybe it was because the gross guy was making a fuss, or maybe it was because she had finally gotten enough sleep, but the girl opened her eyes at the perfect moment.

"...You're so noisy." Fixing her slightly ruffled black hair, she sluggishly righted herself, surveyed her surroundings, and asked, "Oh, was there a winner?"

There was a short silence when nobody spoke. Eventually, I told her the results. "Oh yeah. Fatty won."

The girl's response was simple. After staring up at the sky for a moment, she lightheartedly replied, "Oh, okay. I'm not gonna go out with him, though." Frank, and merciless.

Everything froze. Fatty froze and flopped over like a dead fish; Mr. Perfect got all flustered; the two brothers were, as always, having a lively discourse on workouts; and only one of the men replied to her.

It was Muscleman.

"What are you doing here?"

...Huh?

"Oh, big brother. What brings you here?"

...Big brother?

"Weren't you kidnapped by a group of brawny men?"

"Oh, those were my boyfriends. I was just dating all of them at the same time."

What do you mean boyfriends, plural?

"I see. And now?"

"I was looking for a new boyfriend."

"Did you find one?"

"No luck. All the men have such weak muscles," she said, glancing at Mr. Perfect.

I clapped a hand on Mr. Perfect's shoulder. His face had drained of all color, and he was still crying.

"Um, is this the little sister you told me about?" I asked, just to be sure.

Muscleman nodded. "Yep, this is her."

"......"

What the heck?

○

Having found his little sister at long last, Muscleman returned to his hometown with his sister and her new boyfriend, where they all lived happily ever after.

Huh? Who was her new boyfriend, you ask? Why, it was Mr. Perfect.

"W-wait, please! I've been working hard to gain your brother's approval, so can't you let me go with you?" Wiping tears away as he stepped forward, his gallant figure was a sight to behold. No matter what he did, it was picture-perfect.

The muscle siblings looked at each other.

"Hmm, so you want to build your muscles. I see." Muscleman nodded in understanding, then yawned disinterestedly and let his sister make the ultimate decision.

What does he even see in this girl? Well, they say that love is blind, so I'm sure he'll eventually open his eyes and his heart will cool off. Although by the time that happens, he'll probably be completely muscle-bound.

I waved as the three of them walked into the distance, then heard a strange moan from behind me. *Oh, I forgot about the other guy.*

When I turned around, Mr. Porky was rolling around awkwardly on the ground.

He doesn't exactly inspire me to console him, so let's just leave him there.

"Hey, big brother, what do you think about that pig?"

"Not enough muscles, hey—ah, hey, wait a minute. Our muscle mentor isn't here."

"You're right. He's not here, is he?"

"Don't tell me that he left us here?"

"What do we do?"

"Ahhh!"

The two magician brothers had finally finished their workout discussion. They looked around in confusion at what had happened, and so I generously explained it to them. Blah, blah, yada yada.

"What?! In that case, our muscle mentor has already completed his journey."

"What does that mean for us? This is a grave situation indeed."

"Well, that's how it is," I said. "Miraculously enough, he achieved his ultimate goal." *I'm sure that those three will return to their hometown and live a muscle-bound life. But that's none of my concern, is it?* "Now that you've been released from Muscleman's tutelage, are you two going to go back on tour as magicians?"

The two of them seemed confused by the suggestion.

"Magicians?"

"Magicians?"

Don't tell me. "When I met you two, you were magicians, weren't you? Have you forgotten all about how you used to scam people out of their money?"

"...Ah."

"...Ah."

"That's right... We were magicians..."

"Gah... I'd forgotten because our lives have revolved around working out for so long..."

Muscles are a force to be reckoned with. Well, the two of them have been through a lot.

They remembered who they used to be, and the trio carried on as a troupe of traveling illusionists. And they all lived happily ever after.

......

That's right. As you might have guessed, the third man was Mr. Porky.

"Hey you, why don't you come with us?"

"Yeah, you're on the same wavelength as us. You'll definitely make a good magician."

The two of them each put a hand on Mr. Porky's slumped shoulders and made the suggestion very gently. For his part, Mr. Porky just groaned, covered in snot and without a clue as to what was going on. How unsightly.

But the two brothers seemed to understand.

"Ah, it's all right. Don't worry. We'll teach you everything you need to know."

"From the moment I saw you, I could tell you had a natural gift. Come with us."

Finally, Mr. Porky nodded stiffly.

And thus, the magician trio started their journey. Calling themselves Brothers and the Barrel to avoid the problem of combining their names, these men would soon build a circus guild that would circle the globe.

Or maybe not. I don't know what actually happened.

After all, that story wasn't a part of mine.

CHAPTER 9

Apprentice Witch Elaina

My own story began with a conversation, and I think I remember how it went.

"Congratulations on passing the practical skills exam, Elaina."

"You've become the youngest apprentice witch ever. That's incredible! We're so proud of you!" The two of them were visibly happy for me when I returned home with a bellflower corsage on my breast. But even now, I remember being in a strange state of mind at the time.

I probably sighed heavily and said something like, "But I don't feel very accomplished." I wasn't hiding my embarrassment, I don't think; I'm sure that was how I really felt. I didn't feel like a winner—maybe it didn't even feel real.

In short, I wasn't all that happy.

"Did something happen?" my father asked.

"The others were too weak," I answered. "So it was a bit of a letdown. Now becoming a witch is just a matter of time, I suppose."

"......Oh."

"My, my..."

They didn't know what to say, I think.

I'm certain this conversation is where it started, and what happened afterward was at least partially the fault of my own boastfulness and pride. Those traits would lead me into some troubling situations.

But after all this time, those are all simply memories.

O

It happened about four years ago.

I was fourteen, and I wasn't yet wearing the triangle hat and black robe like I am now. Back then, I usually wore a white blouse and black skirt.

After passing the practical magic exam on my first try, I had decided that I would immediately enter into an apprenticeship under a full-fledged witch. However, for various reasons, I couldn't ask any of the witches who lived in my hometown in the Peaceful Country of Robetta. Well, to be specific, I asked, and they said no.

So I decided to use a secret trick... Well, all I did was listen to the gossip. And according to the rumors—

"I heard that there's a mysterious woman called the Stardust Witch living in the forest near Robetta."

As soon as I heard this, I took off on my broom. *If she's not from Robetta, then maybe she'll accept me as her student,* I thought.

According to the rumors, the Stardust Witch lived deep in the forest; she was a drifter who had settled down of her own accord in an abandoned house above the trees. I only half believed that she existed at all, which was why I was quite surprised when I spied a witch in the forest.

"Oh-ho-ho...ah-ha-ha..."

"......"

Her hair was as black as midnight, she wore a black robe and pointy hat to match, and on her breast was a star-shaped brooch. I could tell from her clothes that this woman living in her secluded forest treehouse was a witch, but not how old she was.

And she was playing with butterflies in the grass.

I gave some serious thought to turning back, but of all the witches I could ask, the strange person before me was the only one remaining. Finally, after some deliberation, I called out to her. "...Um, excuse me?"

She noticed me and tilted her head to the side, still smiling. "Oh-ho-ho... Huh? What's that? Could you be...Elaina?"

I was surprised. We'd never met before; how could she know my name?

"Do you know about me?"

Considering who I was talking to, I had a sneaking suspicion as to the answer, and unfortunately, my hunch was correct.

"Yes, you're rather famous. You're the cheeky brat who completely overwhelmed the competition and passed the practical magic exam at only fourteen, aren't you?"

"……"

"Of course, that's not *my* opinion. I'm sorry if I hurt your feelings."

"…No, I'm used to it."

Since the exam was so strict and only allowed one person to pass each time, as the youngest person ever to pass, I got a lot of attention—negative attention.

After making quick work of mages older than myself, I didn't get along so well with the witches living in my hometown. After they had all turned down my apprenticeship requests, I was here, pinning my hopes on a mysterious witch who lived in the forest.

But if the gossip has made it this far, there's no way she'll accept me. I had already begun to give up.

"Well then, what do you want?"

"…Nothing." I started to leave. I thought it was impossible for sure.

But she said to me, "Might you be here to request an apprenticeship? If so, then I don't mind at all. I've got lots of free time."

"Ah." I was shocked—so much so that I didn't immediately understand what she had said.

"Why are you surprised? Oh, did you come to ask for something else?"

"No, I definitely did want to ask about becoming your apprentice, but…"

"Well, well. Then it's settled. Starting today, you're my apprentice."

"Oh, but…um, huh?" My brain hadn't quite caught up with this strange development. I had expected that if she knew about me, she would refuse me just like the witches in Robetta.

"You seem to have complicated feelings about this. I know what

you're thinking, but relax. I'm not like the weak witches in your hometown. I don't care whether my apprentice is a cheeky brat or not," she
said decisively.

Even now, I remember how her words touched my heart. *Ah, I've
finally managed to find someone who recognizes me for my true abilities*, I
thought.

"Well? Will you become my apprentice? Or will you go grovel to the
weak witches at home?"

I bowed to her. "......I won't be returning home. Please make me
your apprentice."

And that's how I met the Stardust Witch—my teacher, Miss Fran.

Several days had passed since I began my training.

Normal training for an apprentice witch involves learning spells
from her teacher and strengthening her technical skills. Naturally, I
also thought that was what I would be doing.

But my relationship with Miss Fran was a little unusual.

...No, it was *very* unusual. A typical day for me back then went
something like this:

"Good morning, Elaina. I'm hungry, so please make something
to eat."

"...What would you like?" Making Miss Fran's meals for her
became my daily lesson.

"Let's see... I feel like eating steak."

"Isn't that too heavy for first thing in the morning?"

"In that case, those weeds over there will be fine."

"Don't you think that's too far in the other direction?"

Eventually, we would settle on eating bread we had baked the previous day. Then I would study magic on my own until lunchtime. As for
my teacher, she would do some kind of strange research, or go out to
collect edible wild plants, or just generally do as she pleased.

"I'd really like to learn some magic today...," I would say.

"Oh, sorry, I can't step away from this just yet, so could we do it later?" Even when I asked for her help, she usually avoided the issue. Not once did she teach me any spells.

In fact, she encouraged the opposite.

"Elaina, you'll get tired if you study too much. How about enjoying yourself once in a while?"

The conditions that an apprentice witch must meet to become a witch are set by the individual teacher, but exactly what I had to do to earn Miss Fran's approval was completely unclear. She never told me.

All I could do as her apprentice was try my very best. Try what, you ask? Everything, apparently.

I decided that she might not be teaching me magic as a way to foster my independence, and I stopped asking her questions even when there was something I didn't understand. But Miss Fran's demands kept getting more extreme.

"Elaina, we don't have any food. Go buy some."

"Elaina, go into the forest and catch five lizards. I need them for my research."

"Elaina, is dinner ready yet?"

"Elaina, there's a spider in the bathroom. Exterminate it. They scare me."

"Elaina, massage my shoulders."

I told myself that these things were also necessary to become a witch, and day after day I complied with Miss Fran's ridiculous requests like a servant. Looking back on it now, I think I put up with the situation pretty well.

I sometimes doubted her, wondering whether she had just wanted to use me as a servant. But even if I had my doubts, it's not like I could run away. I could try going home, but no one there would become my teacher.

Patience, patience.

I just threw myself into studying and practicing.

One night, before I went to bed, I asked Miss Fran a question.

"Why aren't you teaching me any magic?"

Miss Fran yawned and then answered me nonchalantly, "Because there's no need to teach you."

I didn't understand what she was saying to me at the time.

I endured day after day, and before I knew it, I had spent a month as Miss Fran's apprentice.

It happened while I was going through my nonsensical daily lesson, using wind magic to fell timber and cut it up for firewood, then burning it with fire magic, and finally dousing the fire with water.

"My, my. You're quite reckless, aren't you?"

Miss Fran was standing right behind me. As I recall, this was the first and last time she was ever nearby when I was practicing magic. I stopped what I was doing and rushed over to her. I thought maybe she had finally decided to teach me something.

However, my fleeting hope was smashed in an instant.

"What do you want? I don't really have anything to teach you, you know."

In the end, she really had no intention of teaching me any magic, and she just stayed there behind me watching me practice.

There has to be some meaning to this, I told myself over and over, chanting the words in my heard like an incantation, and earnestly continued my nonsensical routine.

"Before long, it'll be time…," I thought I heard her mumble.

In the afternoon on the following day, she tapped me on the shoulder and said, "I'm going to test you now."

I was taken aback by this sudden announcement and honestly wondered what she was even saying. But more than confused, I felt happy. *I bet if I do well on this test, she'll teach me some magic*, I thought.

Miss Fran led me to a meadow. Lush green grass swayed in the breeze, as far as the eye could see. Standing across from me, she gripped her wand and smiled as she always did. "Starting now, you and I are going to battle."

I was perplexed. Against someone like me, she would be invincible. I was sure of that.

"...Are you joking?"

"Now, now. Do you honestly think I would joke in such a serious situation?"

You haven't taught me one bit of magic, and now suddenly we're battling? This is absurd.

"But Miss Fran, no matter how you look at it, that's..."

"Okay, let's begin."

My weak objections were promptly ignored.

She clapped her hands to give the starting signal and instantly closed the gap between us, where she unleashed a barrage of spells at point-blank range.

I was caught totally off guard and panicked.

The sudden test, the deliberate close-range attacks—thinking back on it now, Miss Fran must have done it on purpose to knock me out of my comfort zone.

It was an underhanded tactic.

"...Eek!" And the Elaina of those days was completely overwhelmed by underhanded tactics.

Spell after spell filled the air, each one a deadly hazard. Balls of magic. Streams of heat. Wind blades. Rock showers. Thunderbolts.

Naturally, I was at a disadvantage in the battle, and it was all I could do just to defend myself. Some of her spells sent me rolling across the grass, others flung me into the air, but all the while I just waited and watched for my chance to counterattack.

"What's wrong? Is that the best you can do? I thought you over-whelmed the others in the practical exam. Not very impressive." Fran spoke gently, smiling her usual smile, even as her relentless attack continued. It was very, very eerie.

It's like she enjoys tormenting me, I thought. *In the end, this woman and the witches back home are exactly the same... She let me become her apprentice just so she could crush me later, didn't she? She didn't teach me anything and neglected me, didn't she?*

During the previous month, I had held doubts in my heart the whole time, but I had deliberately ignored them. *She's different. I can believe in her,* I had told myself so that I could persevere.

"……"

And then everything went black.

When I came to, I was standing still, in a daze. Miss Fran had stopped her attack and sneered at me. "My, my. Done already?"

That was the last straw. A mess of different emotions welled up inside me, and I couldn't hold them in any longer: despair at her betrayal of my trust; frustration at my failure to land a single hit on a fellow witch; sadness at being shunned, avoided, and ignored despite all my work just because I was so young. I couldn't stop them from pouring out of me and smothering my sense of reason. I couldn't take any more of this.

"Urgh…uwaaaaaahhh…"

I cried. I slumped down right where I was standing and started sobbing. I wiped and wiped at my stinging eyes, but the large teardrops wouldn't stop. I tried to bite my lip to keep from wailing and sounding even more pathetic, but I didn't know how to make myself stop. I just sat in the middle of the meadow and cried. I'm sure I was hard to watch.

"Eh? Huh? Um…" Miss Fran looked at me as I cried, her eyes darting around in surprise and confusion. She approached me cautiously. "S-s-s-sorry! I wasn't expecting you to cry…"

Both of her hands moved restlessly as she spoke.

"Waaaaaahhh…"

"Ahhhhhh…"

I didn't want her to see me crying, so I hid my eyes with both hands. Of course, that didn't stop the tears. I bit down extra hard on my lip this time, but I just trembled. Nothing I tried was working; I kept on crying despite my best efforts to stop.

And as for Miss Fran—who knows what she was thinking—she began to search here and there for some way to stem the flow of tears.

"O-okay! …Hey, look here, Elaina. I made one of those butterflies you love!" Fran conjured some ice, whittled it into the shape of a butterfly, and showed it to me. *But I'm not even the one who likes butterflies.*

I continued crying.

"Huh…? It didn't work…? In that case, how about this? A crown made out of weeds!" In a single stroke, she had cut down the weeds growing around us using wind magic, rolled them up, and made them into a crown for me. She tried to put the crown on top of my pointy hat, and I did my best to avoid her.

"N-no good…? Well then, how about this? Look, a fireball!"

I had no idea what she thought that would accomplish.

"I'm running out of options… I'll make funny faces! Look here, hey! Hey!"

I ignored her.

"Um, well then…in that case… Oh yeah!" Finally, after trying every method, she hugged me. It seemed like a desperate measure, something she would only do if there was absolutely nothing else left to try, but it had an instantaneous effect. The swell of my tears and emotions immediately began to recede.

"Mnnn…" I immediately tried to shove her away with all my strength.

"There, there. Calm down, Elaina."

"Stop it…! What—what are you trying to do…?!"

She probably thought I was embarrassed, but that wasn't even close. I was rejecting her embrace because I really, truly hated it. But her arms were coiled around me, squeezing me with surprising strength. There was no getting away.

"I'm sorry, really I am. I overdid it a little bit, didn't I?"

"…Don't joke around! You were having a great time bullying me, and now you want to play nice? You never had any intention of helping me become a witch!"

"Enjoying it? I never…"

"Let me go…! I hate it! I hate everybody! All the witches in Robetta, and you, too! You're all the same! Ugh, and I believed you when you said you were different from the witches at home!"

"……"

"You don't even know how hard I worked! You just see the end result and scoff at it! Why can't just one person see me for who I am?! I'm—I just…I just want approval, but—"

The arms embracing me squeezed tighter.

"I really am sorry, Elaina. I truly understand how you feel." She smoothed my hair. "You've endured everything so well."

"I told you to stop it…! You're trying to fool me again, aren't you?" My voice was wavering.

"No, I'll stop deceiving you. I'll tell you everything. I can't take any more of this, either," she said, placing both hands on my shoulders and looking at me straight on. Her ever-present smile was tinged with sadness.

And then she slowly opened her mouth to speak.

"I did it because I was asked to…by your parents."

○

After we went back to her house in the woods, Miss Fran told me everything.

"It was about a month ago when I met your parents. They handed me this request, along with a large sum of money. 'Please put our daughter through extremely strict training,' it said.

"I had absolutely no idea what they were trying to say, so I tried to ask. Your parents told me they were worried about how you would do going forward. They feared that if you surged ahead as you were, never learning failure, and then lost your way later on, you might find yourself in real trouble.

"Your parents deserve some credit; I want you to understand that they did not make up this plan because they wanted me to bully you, okay?

"They had their own reasons for bringing their plan all the way to someone like me. Your hometown, if I'm not mistaken, is in the Peaceful Country of Robetta, right? The witches who live there are intimidated by your abilities. I heard they all said they couldn't teach a girl like you. After all, that country is very, well…peaceful, so there really aren't any high-caliber witches around…

"So your parents predicted that all the witches in your country would reject you, and so they came to me. To make a long story short, they said you were too full of yourself, and so they thought up a plan to put you through a little hardship early on. Reluctantly, I agreed.

"And then you showed up. Your parents had given me the impression that you were a run-of-the-mill cheeky little brat, so my plan was to be really strict and break your strong will.

"However, when we actually started spending time together, you were nothing like I imagined. You don't balk at whatever effort it takes to achieve your goals, and you have a brilliant and insatiable mind. And the ability to match your ambition. I could have given you my approval right away.

"Since you've been here with me, I've given up on trying to teach the 'Arrogant Elaina' about failure. I'm sure that your parents wanted me to teach you the lesson that 'sometimes things don't go the way you expected,' but I realized that would be pointless.

"It didn't matter how many failures I put you through; I could already see the result. Every single time, you would get back in the fight, and never give up. You would be able to endure any failure. There was no way I could break your will.

"And what's more, there was another issue that I was only able to discover because I am your teacher.

"Elaina, you put up with too much. You're keenly aware of your own youth and your true abilities, so you let me treat you unreasonably.

"No matter how ridiculous I acted, no matter what silly requests I made, you didn't complain at all, did you? After all, you thought there was no one else you could ask to train you, right?

"When you were rejected by the witches of Robetta, what did you think? You gave up on them and set out on your own, didn't you? Did you argue against those witches, even once?

"I decided to wait until you reached the limits of your endurance. And yesterday, when I saw your spells, I guessed it would come very soon. Today's test was the finishing touch.

"By the way, I was expecting the exam to continue until I won, and then, if you still didn't complain, I was planning to lecture you. That would be completely and obviously unfair.

"You can't just hide your true feelings and carry on, because at some point you're going to break. Now, I didn't expect you to burst into tears...but I treated you terribly, didn't I? You're unusually mature, so I completely forgot that you're still a fourteen-year-old girl. I'm truly sorry."

And then Miss Fran added one more thing.

"You mustn't just endure. If you can't stomach it, fight it. Learn to take a stand and say when bad things are bad. Let off steam when you need to. Protect yourself."

I can no longer recall how I felt, hearing my teacher's words, but she told me things in that moment that I had never heard before in my life.

Don't just endure it.

Those words are probably the reason I'm here now. I really think so. Well, even now I have a tendency to let stress build up, though.

O

I trained under Miss Fran for one year. After the warning about persevering too hard in my first month, the true training finally began.

"Good morning, Elaina. I'm hungry, so please make something to eat."

"Here, have some weeds."

"…Um, is this your way of giving me a hard time?"

"I was told not to endure too much abuse, so I decided to try being honest about my feelings. Specifically, the feeling that making breakfast for my teacher is a pain."

"……"

"Just joking."

Eventually, we settled on eating the bread that we had baked the previous day.

As before, I sometimes felt a bit like Miss Fran's servant, but if I thought of it as compensation for all the magic she was finally teaching me, it wasn't painful at all.

Oh-ho, this isn't torture! It's my tuition.

"You have skill and talent," Miss Fran said. "If there's one thing that you don't have, it's experience."

And in order to rectify that, I sparred against Miss Fran over and over. Every day was very enriching.

The many days that I spent there afterward seemed far shorter than the hellish first month. Almost every day we would have intensive magic training, then return to the house in the forest for magic studies. It was so much fun.

During my training with Miss Fran, there was one incident that left an especially deep impression. I was practicing my magic in front of her house in the forest as always.

"Elaina," Miss Fran said abruptly, "there are bottles sitting over there, right? Can you see them?" Sure enough, there were two wine bottles standing where she was pointing.

"Yes, I can see them, but…what about it?"

"Strike one side with a wind spell."

"……"

The distance between the two bottles was about the width of one tree. To be clear, there was plenty of room. There was so much leeway that I thought she was making fun of me.

"Okay." I waved my wand and manipulated the wind. The mass of air made a little *hyoom!* as it went straight for the bottles, hitting one directly, as I had aimed it to do. The bottle flew end over end and landed in the underbrush.

"Okay, I did it."

But Miss Fran shrugged as if to say, "*Good grief.*" "Did I tell you to knock it away?"

"…Uh, but didn't you say to strike it?"

"Let me tell you something. If you're an apprentice witch, you pass the test by knocking it away. But full witches must have more reliable and precise skill than that."

"…Huh."

"A witch doesn't knock down the bottle; she aims for the midway point between knocking it down and not. To put it simply, like this—"

Miss Fran waved her wand, and the wind headed straight for the remaining bottle and hit it directly. However, the bottle did not fall over. It just wobbled around and then stabilized.

Miss Fran smiled. "Oh, good, it worked… All right, just like that. Witches must learn to control their magic precisely. So no more knocking them down."

"……"

I understand what you're trying to say, and it sounds reasonable, but did you have *to go out of your way to make me fail first…?*

After I had spent about a year as her apprentice, I got to the point where I could begin to compete with Miss Fran.

And I was able to win against her—once. That day became the final day of my apprenticeship. Wearing her usual smile, she said, "There is nothing left that I can teach you. You've grown quite strong."

To this day, I can't recall how I was able to win that last time. It was probably just chance. Miss Fran removed the bellflower corsage from my breast and in its place pinned the proof that I was a full-fledged witch.

©Azure

It was a star-shaped brooch.

"Congratulations, Elaina. The Stardust Witch recognizes you as an official witch... By the way, how do you feel about 'the Ashen Witch' for your witch title?"

"...Isn't it a bit too simple?"

Did you decide just by looking at my hair?

"Huh? I thought it was really cool, though..."

"Come to think of it, how did you get the name Stardust Witch, Miss Fran?"

"I chose it because it sounds cool, of course!"

"......"

"Well, how about it? Ashen Witch."

"Sure, that's fine." I didn't particularly care.

"Then it's decided. You are now the Ashen Witch, Elaina. Do your best from now on, okay?"

She clapped a hand on my shoulder.

I inhaled deeply and responded, "I will."

Chatting about the memories we had made during my training, we returned to the house in the woods, and Miss Fran gathered up her luggage right away. She had been a drifter only in name, and in truth she was a distinguished witch from another country. That was the first I had heard of it.

It had been quite difficult to be away from home for a year, she told me with a smile.

That's not really something to smile about..., I thought, but she was probably smiling for my sake.

"In that case, why did you come to the Peaceful Country of Robetta?" I tried to ask her.

"Because there was someone I had to see, no matter what," she replied, refusing to say more. "I would very much like to take my time, but I must be going. There are many people waiting for me back home. That's why this is good-bye."

With that, she turned to leave from the same spot where I had found her chasing butterflies a year earlier.

"Good-bye, Miss Fran." The farewell chilled my body like a glacial wind.

"Good-bye, Elaina. I'll come see you again someday. Please look forward to it and wait for me."

"...Okay!"

And then my teacher got on her broom and flew up into the sky.

I waved and waved as she slowly shrank into the distance, finally disappearing into the blue sky.

That time, I didn't try to hold back my tears.

CHAPTER 10

A Gentle Death Slowly Approaches

In a primeval forest of towering trees, moss grew densely underfoot. Rays of sunlight filtered through the gaps in the vibrant canopy, but the light on the narrow path was dim at best.

I was handling my broom skillfully, avoiding the trees as I proceeded down that path. The lukewarm breeze was very, very uncomfortable against my skin.

"……"

After going just a bit farther, I arrived at a clearing. There was a village there.

A very, very small one. A village so small that you could almost see the whole thing from the entrance.

"Ey."

When I got down off my broom, the moss-covered ground yielded softly to my weight. There didn't appear to be a gate, so I was able to enter the village simply by passing under a trellis.

Wooden houses stood here and there, simple log cabins without a single unnecessary flourish. They appeared to have been built to serve as shelter and nothing more.

Suffice it to say there was nothing remarkable about this village.

Let's not stay here after all—wait, I'm not sure if there's anywhere I could stay the night. Actually, I'm not sure if people are even living here. Is this a ghost town?

I walked aimlessly around the deserted village, and a single villager emerged from one of the houses. *Oh, good, someone does live here.* With some relief, I turned to look at the villager and saw a man in his prime with an ax slung over his shoulder.

"......!"

Strangely, as soon as the man saw me he opened his mouth, dumbfounded, as if he couldn't believe what he was seeing.

......? What could that mean?

My head was tilted in confusion as he pointed a trembling finger at me and shouted, "...Mina! Hey, you're Mina, aren't you?!"

...? Huh?

The man threw his ax down and rushed over to me.

"Thank goodness...! Thank goodness! You found the cure-all, right? You made it just in time! Abel will be so happy, Mina!"

"Huh? Um..."

Immediately, I understood that the man must have me mistaken for someone else. *Who the heck is Abel?*

But just as I was about to open my mouth, the man shouted again.

"Heeey! Everyone! Mina came back!"

In the blink of an eye, his loud voice reached every corner of the village, as if to rouse the primeval forest itself. The trees nearby grew noisy with chattering, and I could see birds making their escape.

It was a really, really small village. If you shouted, everyone in the village would probably be able to hear you. People poured out of their houses in droves.

Old people, children, married couples—when they caught sight of me and the man, the villagers rushed over to us with such nimble, deliberate movements the whole thing felt planned. Before I realized it, I was completely surrounded. *Oh no, this is scary.*

The bustling assembly of people stared at me relentlessly with the kind of pure-hearted admiration usually reserved for heroes returning from war. *Oh no, this is scary.*

"Big Sister Mina! Did you bring back any souvenirs from the city?"

"My, my, you've really become a beauty in the short time you've been gone."

"Did you get shorter?"

"Never mind that, what are you wearing?"

"Come on, Dad. It's obviously the clothing that's popular in the city."

"So did you buy the cure-all?"

"Hey, don't smother her."

The villagers prattled on as much as they pleased.

Ah, I give up, I decided, then tuned out the rest of what they were saying and let the clamoring voices of the villagers wash over me like so much noise. After a bit of time had passed, their cheerful shouts died down.

The man who had summoned all the villagers yelled, "You're all too noisy, be quiet!"

You're the loudest one here. You be quiet.

"…Really, everyone, Mina must be tired from her long journey. Give her a break."

What's this? Now you want to talk like you've got common sense? Aren't you their leader? Wait, more importantly…

"Everyone, I think you're mistaken about something." Now that the crowd had quieted down, I seized the opportunity to speak up and correct them. If the misunderstanding continued any longer, I'd be in trouble.

"Mistaken? About what?" The man looked at me blankly. I could hear a stir spreading through the villagers around me.

I spoke as plainly as possible. "I am simply a traveler. I am not this 'Mina' you're all talking about." I thought I sounded very serious, but it looked like only a few people in the crowd had genuinely listened to what I had to say. Directly behind me, laughter broke out.

"What on earth is the child saying?"

So they won't believe me. What if I use magic to make them kneel down and obey me? Listening to them, I would guess no witch has visited this village, so that in itself should make an impact.

Well, that's a last resort.

"……"

And then, after everyone except for me had had a good laugh, one of the villagers spoke up.

"Hmm? Now that she says that, she does look a little younger than Mina…"

The person next to me chimed in and agreed. "Come to think of it, she's a bit flatter than Mina, too…"

My unease grew steadily greater.

"I thought she had gotten prettier while she'd been gone, but maybe…"

"And if you think about it, growing shorter is completely impossible…"

"And what's with this getup…?"

"Gramma, where's my food?"

"Stop it—you ate just yesterday."

"……"

It took no time at all for my anxiety to wash over me completely. Before I knew it, a dark, funereal atmosphere permeated the crowd.

"…You're really not Mina?" the man in front of me asked miserably.

"I told you that from the beginning. I said you had the wrong person."

"…Then that means"—the man crumpled on the spot, and his voice began trembling—"that we can't do anything to help Abel anymore…?"

"What on earth are you talking about? First of all, who is Abel?"

Ignoring my question, someone muttered, "…No, wait. There's still a way."

Several of the people surrounding me left the circle and huddled together somewhere else, then came back and said, "We have something to discuss with you, so we'd like you to come with us." That was all they would tell me.

Whether because of their amazing powers of persuasion or because the faces of the adults were all deadly serious, I had agreed to go with them before I even realized it.

The man and a number of the other adults brought me to the largest house in the village. We walked into the dining room, where a young man pulled out a chair and said, "Please have a seat." And so I sat.

Two people sat down across from me. The one on the left, from my perspective, was the man in his thirties or so who I had encountered first... He had calmed down, as if the fire in him had gone out, and he suddenly seemed like a different person.

The old man with the white beard sitting to the right (possibly the head of the village) crossed his arms and opened his mouth to speak.

"We understand now that you are not Mina. Our sincerest apologies."

"It's fine." *Understanding that is the first step.*

"However, you look exactly like her; the resemblance was enough that the villagers confused you for her. Just like two peas in a pod, you could say."

The thirtyish man nodded vigorously.

The old man stroked his beard. "First, let us make our request. Traveler, just for one night—even less than one night, in fact—could you please pretend to be Mina?"

"...Why?"

I had an inkling that it might have to do with the famous Abel.

"Mina had a boyfriend. His name is Abel, and he's very serious, very kind. For his sake, we'd like you to put on a little performance."

Called it. Shall we try to guess the next plot twist?

"Abel's life is in danger, so you want me to pretend to be his girl-friend coming home after moving to the city?"

But the old man shook his head slowly. "No, Mina did not move away to live in the city. She ran off to get the cure-all."

"...Hmm." Come to think of it, the villagers and the man in his prime had said the same thing about getting some cure-all.

"Right now, Abel is lying in his sickbed."

"…Mm," I urged him on.

"What's destroying Abel seems to be an incurable disease. It's bad enough to make the village doctor want to throw in the towel. No matter what type of medicine he administers, it has absolutely no effect. In fact, Abel's condition actually gets worse. At first, he just had a simple fever, but now he can't even stand upright."

I see. "And so this cure-all?"

"Mm. Right after we realized the medicine we had in the village wasn't doing him any good, Mina flew off, saying, 'I'm going to get the cure-all.'"

"And where can one acquire this cure-all?"

"If you proceed far to the north from here, there is a large country. Rumor has it you can acquire the cure-all there, but it's a full two days' walk. No one from this village has been there to confirm whether it's true or not."

"So Mina dashed out of the village, relying on that questionable information."

"She must have been willing to take the risk. She wanted so much to help Abel, but…" The man in his thirties finished the rest of that sentence weakly, hanging his head. "Two weeks have passed since she left here. Mina—my daughter—should have come back long ago, but she hasn't returned."

…Daughter? Did he say daughter?

"Huh, are you her father?" This was a surprise. The man in his thirties nodded quietly. *It's pretty bad to honestly confuse your own daughter and a complete stranger… Well, he must be very exhausted.*

"The more time passes, the closer Abel comes to death," the old man said. "The village doctor is saying that at most he has three days left."

Three days. Will Mina make it back in time?

It takes two days to arrive at the country that has the cure-all, then another two to buy the medicine and come back. But it's already been two weeks.

Returning ten days late (and counting) was really something else. I couldn't help but think she had run into some kind of trouble—or worse. Could Mina possibly make it back before his time was up? No, the two people seated in front of me were already sure of one thing.

Mina is never coming back...

"Up until now, Abel was fighting his sickness with everything he had, but...his girlfriend was by his side like family the whole time. If he dies without being able to see her, it would be unbearably sad."

"......"

"Ever since he lost his family when he was small, Mina has been the only one who supported him. And Mina's the only one who can ease his mind. A fake Mina will do—we just want you to make him feel happy at the end, at least," said the old man.

○

Even though I hadn't agreed at first, I eventually decided to go along with the old man's suggestion. There was no risk to me, and I would have been an awful person to refuse at that point.

That said, I was a traveler. I didn't want to spend a whole day in a dull village with no inn in sight. If possible, I wanted to get on my broom and hurry to the country that was said to have the cure-all medicine.

That was why I presented my conditions up front. "I'll cooperate. But only once. After I meet Abel, I'm resuming my travels immediately."

The two of them said that would be fine. Once that was decided, we hurried to prepare. I was taken from the big house to another house, where several girls and women from the village awaited me. They varied widely in age, from young girls to old women.

Among them, one particularly elderly woman seemed to be the person in charge. Small wrinkles lined her face as she spoke. "All right then, let's get ready. Men, get out!"

In an impressive display of violence, the women in the house began using sticks to beat back all of the village men who had come to see the spectacle, including the old man and Mina's father, and took complete control.

The old woman closed the door and barred it so that no one could enter, then signaled the rest of them with her eyes. When she did, everyone but me started closing every curtain in the house and the back door.

Once the house was dark, the old woman approached me. "Take 'em off." She was suddenly holding a robe.

"I'm sorry?"

"Hurry up and take those strange clothes off! If you go looking like that, Abel will know you aren't her!"

Oh, so that's what you mean. I wasn't expecting that.

I took care to remove the precious brooch that proved I was a witch from my robe. With it still in my hand, I stripped down to my underwear.

A very young girl politely took the clothes I removed off to the side to fold them.

"Okay, have her put this on."

Another girl took a package from the old woman and hurried over to me, then took the clothes out. "All right, everyone. I'm going to put this on the traveler, so help me out."

Huh? I can dress myself.

But before I could respond, a crowd of women was already bearing down on me from all sides. There was nothing I could do but shut my mouth.

Thus, I became a dress-up doll.

"Okay, lift her leg."

"Would you put her arm through the sleeve of this blouse? Uh-oh, it's the wrong size."

"She really is the spitting image of Mina."

"She's even prettier than Mina."

"Yeah."

"What color is good for the ribbon? Oh, red, of course."

Everyone seemed a little too enthusiastic to me. I could have sworn they were just doing this for fun.

After the dressing was more or less finished, I looked down and found I had been dressed in a white blouse and an olive-brown flared skirt. *I could have put something like this on myself, though...*

"All right, time for the finishing touches. Miss Traveler, this might hurt a bit, but hang in there, okay?" As she spoke in a cheerful tone of voice, the woman behind me wrapped something black around me.

"......?"

And what do you think it was? A corset. Before I knew it, the thing was around my torso.

"Huh, um, hold on a—"

Ignoring my bewilderment over the sudden turn of events, the girls surrounding me grabbed my body and yanked the strings at my back with all their might. It felt like my rib cage was being crushed.

"Th-that hurts! Ow! If you have to tighten it, at least do it more gently!"

"Oh, come on. Don't struggle."

"Persevere, persevere."

"You'll get used to it soon."

"Do your best, Miss Traveler."

With that, the work of changing my clothes came to an end, and everyone seemed satisfied except for me.

Afterward, the old woman said, "It looks like you don't have enough of a chest, so let's stuff it a bit, shall we?" and held out wads of cotton to me. Apparently, she was serious. I slapped them to the floor.

©Azure

O

There was a small house on the edge of the village.

It looked completely unattended, and as I walked over, I crushed knee-height grass noisily underfoot. Compared to the other houses clustered together, this small house was old. You could probably punch right through the thin planks of its walls with a single hit. It looked less like a house where someone would live and more like a rarely used storehouse.

They told me Abel was quarantined here.

Abel had suddenly fallen ill one day, and the villagers didn't know whether or not his disease was contagious. That's why they had shut him up in this small house, to reduce the possibility of spreading it. Apparently, Mina's father had been taking care of him. At first, his girlfriend had been nursing him from morning until night, but she had left the village when his condition took a turn for the worse.

Some villagers wondered whether Mina might have run away, but no one knew whether that was true or not.

After taking a few deep breaths in front of the hut, I opened the door. It made a squeaking sound that hurt my ears.

"......"

I went inside and closed the door with a hand behind my back.

A man was lying on the bed. He was young, and he had black hair. It was easy to see that his face was handsome back when he was healthy—but now he was a shadow of his former self. The man turning his vacant eyes toward me had sunken cheeks and no light behind his eyes.

"...Mina?" His lips moved slightly, forming the name of his beloved.

"Yes. It's me," I lied. "Have you been well?"

The floorboards squeaked underfoot as I moved to sit in the chair to the side of the bed.

He smiled faintly. "You came back... I thought—I thought I'd never see you again."

"I'm your girlfriend. Of course I was going to come back, no matter what."

"...Of course."

He stared out the window.

There was nothing there. Just overgrown weeds and the primeval forest in the distance. The small hut didn't just appear decrepit; it was truly falling apart, and a draft that blew in from somewhere rustled the man's hair.

"I found the cure-all medicine," I told him, as if I was reading from a prepared script. "I'm going to bring it along with your dinner tonight, so please take one pill after eating plenty of food. It may take some time, but you should definitely get better." This, too, was a lie.

Mina's father had written the speech. He thought it would be suspicious if Mina came back without the cure-all, so he had me act as if I had the medicine in hand, to reassure Abel.

The pill I was bringing with dinner contained sleeping medication. They would have him talk to his beloved in his last moments, and after that, the villagers would do something with him—they hadn't told me what. There had been no need to ask.

"Say, Mina." He looked into my eyes. "Would you hold my hand?" With heavy movements, he stuck a hand out from under his quilt. It was not the muscled hand of a young man, but withered and bony.

I mustn't falter.

I immediately grasped it with both hands. It was so cold, it was hard to imagine any blood was flowing through it at all.

"So warm...my blood must already be growing cold...," he said. "Say, Mina," he called the name of his beloved. "Would you give me a kiss?"

"Huh, a kiss?" I asked involuntarily. I immediately felt intense regret.

"...Yes, a kiss. Do you not want to?" I thought I saw a dim flash of suspicion in the depths of his eyes. I thought hard. *What should I do? If I'm his girlfriend, then of course, I ought to kiss him, but I'm— Ahhh, if I hesitate, he's going to be suspicious. What to do, what to do...?*

He looked at me as I floundered, and chuckled.

"Sorry, I was just teasing. Please don't mind it." Somehow, he looked like he had recovered just a little bit of his energy.

After that, he smiled and said, "I'm not going to pester someone who isn't my girlfriend for a kiss."

I was upset by the idea that he had spotted the deception due to some imperfection in my performance, and I denied the charge many times over, but he was sure.

"You're not the real Mina. You don't need to force it," he said confidently, despite my efforts to continue my act. "First of all, it's not like Mina's even going to come back to me. I'm such a fool."

I wasn't sure who he was speaking to, but I suspected something else was going on here. I gave up pretending to be Mina and revealed everything about myself—that I was a traveler, that I was a witch, that I had been asked to pretend to be Mina because we looked alike. I hid nothing.

"Hmm," he said, "you really are the spitting image of Mina."

"We look that similar, huh?"

"Yeah. You could say you're two peas in a pod. But...," he asked, "...what's a witch?"

"The people of this village really don't know about witches, do they?"

"No, this is the first I've heard of them."

Well, I suppose it's not impossible for them not to know about witches, since this is a remote village two full days' travel from the nearest country. I explained in detail, producing my wand and performing some magic so it would be easy for him to understand.

"Amazing...! Ha-ha, I never knew such people even existed!"

Abel laughed, making his best effort to speak loudly. His dry laugh soon got caught in his throat, where it turned into a cough.

"Are you all right?"

"Yeah, sorry. I got a little overexcited. Well then, concerning Mina and me..."

"…Right. What happened? You said she wouldn't be coming back."

He looked up at the ceiling. "I made up the story about the cure-all. It doesn't exist."

"It doesn't exist…?"

He nodded. "Mina was…"

And then he quietly told me the story.

"She was really kind, and cute, and good. She was wasted on me. She was the only one who supported me.

"Even after I fell ill, she took care of me and never acted as if the task was unpleasant. She came to my room every day, gave me homemade food to eat, and brought books so that I wouldn't get bored after I was bedridden. She sat by my side until I slept. She was my lifeline, tending to me with all her heart.

"But my illness just kept getting worse—it didn't matter how much medicine they gave me or how much I rested. Soon, I couldn't eat properly. Mina brought me her home-cooked meals, and I still couldn't muster up an appetite. In fact, I felt like I would throw up. It was obvious that I couldn't hold on much longer. I could tell.

"But she tried her hardest to cheer me up. I adored her, but I also felt terrible for her. She wanted so desperately for me to live on.

"One day, I said to her, 'My illness can't be cured by the medicine we have in the village. I'm not getting better. Do you know of the large country two days north of here? I've heard they have a medicine that's effective against any kind of illness. If it's all right, would you go get it for me?'

"Mina was perplexed. She wondered if such a cure truly existed. Besides, I was sure to get better if I just tried, she said.

"I ignored her. Instead, I pressed into her hands a letter and the money I had saved for the two of us to someday go on a trip together, and I said, 'You should be able to buy it with this. Bring it to me. Don't you dare come back until you have that cure-all in your hand. As for that letter, open it if you can't find the medicine and you really have no idea what to do.'

"Mina was really a good girl. After worrying and worrying, she eventually got on board with my plan. 'I will find it and come back to you; you can count on it,' she said. But in reality, there was no such medicine.

"The following day, my surroundings changed. Mina left to find the cure-all, and bit by bit, word spread through the village that my condition was deteriorating. Some people came out and said my illness might be contagious, and the end result was this. I was quarantined, and only Mina's father attended to me. But that's fine with me.

"…I really, really love Mina. I love her so much it hurts. Of course, it's painful to be so far apart, but even more than that, I hate that I'm making her sad. I don't want her crying over my corpse. I want her to smile as much as possible. That's why I decided to send her away from the village.

"If I had said, 'It's best if you don't come see me anymore,' she would never agree, I knew. Even if I managed to turn her away so that she wouldn't come to my side anymore, she would have been heartbroken, of course. And I didn't want the other villagers to get involved.

"Above all else, I didn't think she could truly live happily in the village where my dead body was put to rest. It's a conceited thing to think, I know, but I imagined that she might be weighed down by my memory.

"I'm certain she reached the country two days' walk from here and searched for the cure-all there. I'm sure that she walked around the country for hours, days on end to no avail. And I'm sure she then opened my letter.

"I poured all of my feelings into that letter. I told her I would surely be dead by the time she read it, and that I wanted her to be happy somehow in the new country.

"I believe she'll be able to find a wonderful man in that big country who can heal her wounded heart. There must be someone who can make her smile again.

"It's so selfish, isn't it? But that's what I had been thinking for a while. She was meant for more than a cramped village like this. She ought to see the wider world.

"By the way, Miss Traveler, if you're pretending to be Mina, that must mean she hasn't returned, right? I believe two weeks have passed since she left the village.

"In that case, it must have happened. She must have found happiness."

After his story was done, the sick man looked out the window with tired, vacant eyes. The wind blew; the withered leaves danced and, finally, fell.

"Are you all right with that?" They were trite words, but I couldn't find anything better to say to him.

"Of course not. It's a sad thing to be apart from the one you love."

"……"

In that case—, I was about to say, but I stopped myself.

Both Mina and Abel were sad to be apart, but they would have to overcome it. And they seemed to be doing their best to make it through. An outsider shouldn't butt in to such a private matter.

"I'm glad I met you, Miss Traveler. You're not really Mina, but I still feel like I got to see her one last time."

"…I'm also glad I got to meet you."

"That's good…," he mumbled, and then said, "Miss, you're a wandering witch. Does that mean you have mysterious magical powers?"

"Hmm? Yes, I do." I was a little surprised by the sudden question, but I answered in the affirmative. Magic isn't something that just anyone can deal in, after all.

"The magic you showed me earlier truly was amazing. It was like being in a dream world."

"Thanks for saying so. I'm happy you enjoyed it."

"Say, what else can you do with magic? For example, could you—?"

○

I left the hut and went straight back to the house where I had changed clothes. Then I had the crowd of women take the corset off. They had tied the back too tightly for me to take it off myself.

"Did it go well?" the old woman asked me after I had changed back into my robe.

I gave a phony answer. "Yes. He never suspected a thing."

"Thank goodness. He must have been happy to be able to see Mina in his final hours."

"......"

His final hours?

"So what is Abel doing now?"

"He was tired from talking after so long, so he said he was going to sleep. Please leave him alone until tonight."

"I see. Understood. I'll tell the village headman, too."

The village headman must be the old man with the white beard. "Please do."

I put on my star-shaped brooch and my pointy hat, and my transformation was complete. I had returned to my usual self.

"What will you do now? If you're staying in the village, my house is open to you, but..."

I was happy for the suggestion, but I shook my head. "No, thank you. I'm going to leave the village now. I'm in a hurry to get going." *Also, I want to try to make it to that big country.*

"...That's too bad."

"I'm sorry."

"You're leaving without seeing the headman and the others?"

"If I saw them, they would probably try to stop me, right? I should just slip away. If you see the headman and Mina's father, please give them my regards."

"Going so soon?" said one of the girls who had helped me out of my corset.

"Too bad," commented another girl.

"Come again, okay?"

As for me: "Sure, I'll definitely come back," I mumbled halfheart-edly.

And so I left the village. I flew north, straight through the primeval forest, and didn't look back. My hand was gripping the broom, but I could still feel Abel's cold fingers.

And he...

O

"...Are you seriously asking me that?"

I was extremely perplexed after listening to his proposal.

"Yes, I'm serious... I'm going to die soon, right? I have no doubt that the end is near for me. It's unbearably frightening. Day after day I fall asleep thinking that today could be the day I don't wake up. It's terrifying, and I can't do anything about it." From where he lay on the bed, he continued, "Besides, I know. Everyone in the village, even Mina's father, doesn't have any sympathy for me. Somewhere deep in their hearts, they're all hoping for my death. When I finally die, they won't have to take care of me anymore, they're thinking. I can't take it anymore. I'm at my limit. That's why... Can I ask you...? Can I ask you to kill me?"

He wasn't joking.

He was speaking seriously.

He was already at his limit.

However...

"I refuse."

There was no way that I could accept such a request. I didn't become a witch to kill people. Even if it was his final request, I couldn't do it.

"...That's too bad." He was calm; I think he had never expected me to accept in the first place.

"I'm sorry."

"No, you don't need to apologize. Even if you don't kill me, the villagers will do it themselves before long. Maybe even tonight. They'll feed me poison or something, and it'll look like I just quietly drifted off."

"...No way."

"No, I'm sure of it. A person who just lies in bed and can't get up has no worth in this village. He can't do anything except wait for death."

"......"

"The only reason I've been able to hold on until now is because the villagers were expecting Mina to come back. They were convinced that she had a lingering attachment to me...but it's all over now."

I realized what he meant...

"...And then I showed up."

"Don't misunderstand me. I'm not really blaming you, okay? This was my fate sooner or later."

"......"

And then he smiled.

"Ideally, I would pass away while Mina's twin is tending to me, but...I don't want to force your hand. I'm sorry for making such a strange request."

"No, don't worry about it...," I said.

CHAPTER 11

The Country That Persecutes Ugliness

A forest path cut through a stretch of nearly uniform trees. It was unpaved and uneven, little more than a gap where no trees grew.

Above it flew a single girl on her broom. The swaying branches whispered as she passed by, and the trees tossed their leaves into the air as if they were celebrating a toast.

The lovely young lady was a witch and a traveler.

Her ashen hair shimmered in the sunlight, and her lapis lazuli eyes seemed to be gazing beyond her path to somewhere far into the distance. She wore a black robe, a pointy hat, and a brooch shaped like a star, and it wouldn't be an exaggeration to say that her witchy appearance only added to her appeal.

This young lady, who no one could possibly describe as anything other than lovely…who could she be?

That's right. She's me.

"……"

I had already gotten some information about the country that was supposed to lie ahead. Among the merchants who made their living in this area, that country was called all sorts of strange names: "the big yet small country," "the country of only handsome men and beautiful ladies," "the walled country," "the old-fashioned country," "the forbidding country," "the curious country," and so on. I had come to wish that they would at least be a little more consistent.

Anyway, the only thing I was certain of was that a strange place lay before me. I wondered just what kind of strangeness it had in store for me, and what made it so mysterious. I had tried asking the merchants, but it was no use. In the end, if I wanted to know what the place was really like, there was nothing to do but go there and check it out myself. I was kind of looking forward to it.

A bit more time passed, and my destination appeared on the horizon. I could make out a relatively low rampart, and the wooden gate was standing open.

I parked my broom in front of the gate and dismounted.

A guard appeared out of nowhere and began with an overenthusiastic greeting. "Hey there— Oh, a witch? How unusual." He looked at the brooch on my chest, and his eyes grew wide. "What brings you to these parts?"

"I am a traveler."

"Oh-ho, that's even more unusual."

"Is that so?"

The guard nodded two or three times. "Indeed. By the way, Madam Witch, do you know anything about this country?"

"Well, I know a fair bit."

"Oh really? In that case, I'm sure it'll be all right."

"...?" *Wait, what will be all right?* I was confused.

"Well then, Miss Witch, please answer a few simple questions before you come in. First of all..."

The standard questions dispelled whatever slight doubts I was feeling. The questions he asked me were ordinary things like my name, my age, how long I planned to stay, and the reason for my visit. I gave succinct answers.

"All right, that's all we need. You're free to enter."

"Thanks."

At the guard's urging, I stepped into a new land.

Well then, what kind of place is this?

O

Just going on a stroll wouldn't be enough to show whether this country was as odd as I'd heard. Stepping through the gate, everything appeared exceptionally ordinary, although it would have been more appropriate to call the place a walled village rather than a country of any description.

Most everything was built of wood, and every house appeared to have been made from rough timber. Most likely, people had simply cleared the path I had just traveled down and used the trees to build houses. The problem was that all of them were falling apart. They were so shabby that they looked like they'd had an encounter with the Big Bad Wolf.

By the way, the people living in the houses…were pigs!

…No, they were human, of course.

A thin woman emerged from one of the houses, holding a basket. After looking at me for only a moment, she turned and left.

What a perfectly disinterested reaction. Looks like visitors aren't that rare after all.

It wasn't just the woman holding the basket. Everyone I encountered seemed utterly indifferent. Or maybe I should say utterly ordinary.

There was the woman hanging her laundry to dry on a pole between two trees in a garden. There were the men sitting around a bonfire in the distance, having a friendly chat and tossing branches into the flames. There was the young man who was intensely focused on chopping firewood with an ax.

I saw the residents of the country from a distance, but as soon as they met my gaze, they would turn their eyes away, as if they were thinking, *Oh, a traveler. Ho-hum.*

Just as I had been told, they all seemed to be handsome men and beautiful women, and they were probably a bit old-fashioned. However, at present, I had no feelings about the land aside from finding it totally ordinary and rather boring. *Not exactly living up to the reviews, is it?*

"My, my, how rare."

As I was walking around aimlessly, someone called out to me. I looked in the direction the voice had come from and saw an older woman, clearly a mage, walking toward me. When my eyes met hers, she grinned. It was a smile brimming over with a certain enigmatic kindness. Judging by her appearance, she was probably about the same age as my parents.

I looked behind me just in case she was speaking to someone else. After I was sure I wasn't about to embarrass myself, I asked, "Me?"

The woman nodded. "Yes, you. You're a traveler, right? If you came to this country, you must have really strange tastes."

"Is that so?"

"Quite."

"I heard it was a strange place, so it caught my interest."

"Hmm, you're an odd one."

"Is that so?"

"Quite."

This mage had inexplicably struck up a friendly conversation, then accused me of being an odd person with strange tastes. *What's going on? I don't understand.*

"But it doesn't look very strange at all. I think it's just a plain, ordinary, normal place."

"Incidentally, what did you hear about us before you came here?"

"Um…" I told her the different names that the merchants were calling this country.

"…Hmm. 'The country of only handsome men and beautiful ladies,' huh… Oh-ho-ho, I'm blushing."

"……" *Are you only hearing the parts you want to hear?*

"Well then," the mage said, "you came with high expectations and were disappointed, is that right?"

"Yes, well, something like that."

"…I see. In that case, I think you should come look at the interior. I suspect you'll be able to find what you were hoping for."

"The interior…? What do you mean?"

"I mean just what I said. Come with me."

"Um, hang on—"

She grabbed my sleeve tight, and I found myself being dragged along by a mage whose name I didn't even know.

…Why me?

She led me to a gate.

This wasn't the gate that I had gone through to enter the village, but a more extravagant one. The top of the wooden gate was adorned with an iron frame. Somehow, this rampart seemed taller than the wall I had seen when I had first entered.

The gate was open, and a horse-drawn cart was parked to one side. Fat older men were unloading packages of all sizes while the horse munched on grass for lack of anything better to do.

What in the world is this?

"…Is there another country inside this country?" I asked, and the mage released my sleeve.

"Yes. Although the territory on the other side of this gate is the real country."

"In that case, what's on this side?" I pointed at the ground.

"I'll tell you if you listen to what I say."

"……" *I have a bad feeling about this.*

"You won't do business with me?"

"Is this a business transaction?"

"Quite."

"Depends on what you have to say," I said, and the mage's eyes glittered as if to say, "*Got it.*"

"Go buy me a book. I'll give you the money."

"…A book?" I thought she was going to ask for something crazy, but that was a very normal item. "Why don't you buy it yourself? Or is there some reason why you can't buy it?"

"Yes, I have a reason. Can I count on you?"

I was about to ask what the reason was, but I could tell from the look in her eyes that she would only dodge the question and promise to tell me after I brought her the book.

Well, if it's just a simple errand, that should be all right.

I didn't feel good about letting this mage foist her errand onto me, but I was also very curious about what was on the other side of that gate.

"I accept."

O

I slipped past the sluggish-looking horse and the fat men and went through the secondary gate.

Inside was a whole other world, so different it made me wonder what on earth was the deal with the backwoods hamlet I had passed through before.

The bare, unpaved earth I had been walking on…was no more. Solid-looking rust-colored bricks were lined up to form the road.

No, they don't just look *solid, they* are *solid.*

The houses built along the gently winding road were also made of brick instead of wood. They would be sure to stand up to any huffing, puffing wolf.

As I walked on, the aroma of coffee reached my nose, and I spotted a café. A number of people inside were smiling at me.

Proceeding onward, I saw a bakery, just the type I love. This country didn't seem to have any street stalls or any other roadside businesses. The bakery itself was set up inside an ordinary house. *Come to think of it, I haven't eaten anything since this morning.*

But I should take a look around before I put anything in my mouth. Besides, since I went to the trouble of coming here, I want to eat something this place is famous for.

"Hey, hey, Mom, there's an uggo over there. Look how ugly she is!"

"Shh! Don't look."

......

...Huh? What was that just now?

When I turned toward whoever had made that very, very rude comment, an obese mother and child were holding hands and wrinkling their noses at me in disgust.

Did they just say that about me? The mother and child met my eyes as they walked away, and the child started to holler.

"Eek, the uggo glared at meee!"

"Hey, stop looking! You'll turn ugly!"

......What in the world is going on?

I puzzled over it, but no answer was forthcoming. Eventually, I concluded that I had been imagining things.

The farther I went, the worse it got.

Or should I say, the more people I passed, the more disapproving eyes turned my way. People sometimes said it while pointing at me and sneering, and sometimes while whispering to the person next to them.

Ugly, they said.

"Oh, my word! It hurts to look!"

"Goodness, what an awful face. She shouldn't show that to anybody."

"How dare she walk around like nothing's wrong? Have some respect."

"Too thin."

"That girl looks like a skeleton."

"She's a bad influence on the children. Can't someone make her go away?"

"But she's a witch."

"Ah, she is. An ugly witch."

Well, you get the picture.

As you would expect, I didn't mind one bit that I seemed to be upsetting them.

"*What, are you jealous?*" I wanted to say to them. But when you're walking through an environment where open discrimination is socially acceptable, it's natural to expect objectionable things to happen.

For example, having a man (who resembles a bloated hog) laugh at you.

"Hya-ha-ha! She's far too hideous! She looks just like a servant!"

For example, frightening an old geezer (who resembles a bloated hog).

"Eek! It's the grim reaper! Don't tell me… Is it my time…?"

For example, having a child (who resembles a bloated hog) throw stones at you.

"Get outta here, uggo!"

Children don't throw very hard, at least, so the stones were easy enough to dodge.

Incidentally, I used air magic to blow him away on the wind. It helped me let off a little stress, and he had so much fat on his body that I don't think he was in any danger.

But the unpleasantries did not end after my modest revenge.

"Hey, you're in the way, damn uggo," someone snarled, slamming her shoulder into me as she went by.

What beautiful specimen might have declared me an uggo this time?

When I turned around to look, there was a large, fleshy woman.

Wow, what wonderful meat. She looks just like a sow ready for market.

To put it another way, she was an extremely fat young lady with an extremely porcine face. Her perfectly rotund body was clad in a frilly dress, and she walked down the center of the road wearing an expression of pride.

Yet she was being showered with praise.

"My, what a beauty!"

"Now that's what a girl ought to look like."

"Isn't she a little too fat?"

"That's the best. Don't you get it?"

"How incredible... I want her for my wife."

"Compared to her, what's with that witch?"

"That witch is all skin and bones."

"Too skinny."

That's about how it went. I found it very, very unpleasant that their comments somehow spread to include me.

"...Phew."

For the time being, I returned to the road I had come in on and burst into the coffee shop. I had to flee. It was too uncomfortable.

"Welcome. What'll you have? ... *Tch*," a man with a doglike face (fat, of course) asked me, a creepy smile spreading over his lips.

"Um, I'll have the breakfast set." I chose the first thing on the menu. And the cheapest.

"Certainly." The waiter hurriedly left my side and started whispering about something with another waiter.

Well, I suppose they're making fun of my appearance.

"......"

It wasn't important enough to think about, or to say anything about. *What is the deal with this country?* Beyond the second gate, the concept of ugliness was quite different than usual.

"Hey, look...an uggo's sitting over there."

"You idiot! Be careful when you talk about the uglies. What if you get infected?"

"C-crap...sorry!"

"Sheesh..."

Leaving aside the issue of whether ugliness was contagious, even here inside the coffee shop, the other customers were glaring daggers at me. I really didn't understand it at all, but it seemed that I was the target of some local prejudice.

"Apologies for the wait. Here is your morning set." The waiter looked down his nose at me as he set down coffee and bread. And jam.

A very modest set. As expected for the cheapest thing on the menu.

Still smiling his creepy smile, the waiter said, "Pardon the request, miss, but when you have finished eating, would you please leave the shop right away? We've had complaints from other guests, so…"

"Um…"

I heard laughter from one of the seats.

After finishing my breakfast extremely slowly and delicately, I headed for a bookstore.

I can't deny that I wanted to run away as quickly as I could, but I had made a promise, so I couldn't leave just yet. I reluctantly walked through the town, intently keeping my gaze ahead as yet more people pointed and laughed, until finally I arrived at the bookstore.

Inside, the store was nearly silent—as one would expect on such sacred ground. The ladies and gentlemen inside the shop (all fat, without exception) were absorbed in searching the shelves or reading the books they had in hand and did not so much as acknowledge me.

A safe space.

"Hmm…" I drifted around the shop trying to remember the title of the book the mage had asked me to get. After a while, I found it. It was displayed faceup in the new publications corner. I took one copy and headed for the counter.

"Welcome." The clerk took the book with an appropriately polite attitude. "Shall I put a cover on it?"

"Yes, please."

The clerk wasn't openly rude to me, but I imagined she was probably laughing at me on the inside.

…With nothing to do for a moment, I looked away and saw a pile of rather tasteless bookmarks on the counter. Looking closer, they were taxidermy spiders, crushed flat. They had THIS IS A BOOKMARK written on them, so the disgusting things were indeed bookmarks. No doubt about it.

"Ah, could I ask you to stick one of these bookmarks in every fifty pages?"

"You sure have bad taste, huh?"

Well then, why are they even here?

Just as I was leaving the bookstore, a group of adults surrounded me. I didn't know what they were saying to me, nor exactly what had happened. The crowd was made up of people (all fat, without exception) I had encountered earlier.

"Hey, you're that traveler who sneaked in here, right?" one of the fat men asked.

I tried to remember who he was, and then I realized he was one of the men who had been unloading packages from the horse cart near the second gate earlier.

"Sneaked in?" *That's awfully presumptuous.*

"You slipped by while we guards were bringing in packages from outside, right? You know ugly people aren't allowed to enter this part of the country. What, were you trying to spite us?"

"Huh?" *They aren't allowed?*

"Don't play dumb. When you went through the first gate, the guard on your side should've explained it. The second gate marks a special place where only select people may enter. To willingly break this rule is an extremely malicious act."

"Uh-huh." Sure enough, I remembered the guard at the first gate asking me whether I knew anything about this land.

"How can you take that attitude with us? You're causing the residents a lot of trouble just by being here. Hurry up and get out."

"You don't have to tell me. I was just about to leave." *I already finished my errand.*

"…Humph, don't come back."

No need to worry. I wouldn't come here again even if you begged me, I nearly replied. But since I'm not stupid enough to pour oil on a fire, I just said, "Yes, of course," and left it at that.

O

"My, my, you're finally back."

I had returned to the old-fashioned village surrounding the flourishing interior city.

She was waiting for me in front of the secondary gate as I came out. I was glad she saved me the effort of looking for her, but I got the feeling that everything, even down to the timing of when I would go meet her, had been predicted somehow. As if I'd been playing right into her hands the whole time.

It was probably my imagination.

"Hello. I got the book, as promised."

"Great, thank you." She moved to take it from my hands.

"But first, would you tell me about this place? I'll give it to you afterward," I said, holding the book high in the air.

She pulled back her hand. "Fair enough. Okay, shall we go somewhere where we can sit down?"

Then she led me to a particularly nondescript bench. It had clearly been standing there for a long time. Moss grew around its legs, the planks were riddled with holes, it creaked when I sat down. I was a little scared I might go crashing through the seat at any moment.

My heart pounded as if I was holding a ticking time bomb, but the mage ignored me and gazed out at the quiet, tranquil scenery. "It's much better out here than it is in there, right? It's peaceful."

"...Well, I suppose so."

Though don't you think it's a little too *peaceful?*

"What did you want to ask?"

"I think you already know, don't you?"

The mage was quiet for a little while. And then, she told me the story in fits and starts. "—Long ago, when this land was not yet divided, there was a very ugly queen."

"An ugly queen?" I tilted my head, silently asking, "*Ugly by whose standards?*"

"Well, the people on the other side of that gate would have called her beautiful, but the queen was ugly by your sensibilities."

"You're not pulling any punches, eh?"

"It's simply the truth."

"......"

"To get back to the story, the queen always felt inferior because she was so ugly. In those days, everyone thought that queens ought to be beautiful, so she was very timid about her appearance."

Mm-hmm...?

The mage continued talking. "And so, the queen made a request of a certain wandering witch. 'Make my face beautiful,' she said. However, the witch refused. She didn't know any spells for changing people's faces; plus, she thought it would be unethical."

"And that wandering witch was you?"

She shook her head. "No. I'm simply a mage. Look, I don't have a brooch or anything, do I?" She tugged on the front of her robe and showed it to me. As she said, there was nothing there.

"Then how do you know that the queen asked the wandering witch to do that?"

"Because I'm friends with her. We hit it off when she came to this country, although we were only together for a short while. She was a traveler, after all."

"Ah."

"She and I were just about the same age as you are right now, and she looked just like you. She was very smart and very beautiful."

"Ahhh..."

Is she trying to flatter me? I'm not so sure...

"Anyway, the witch declined the queen's request. Apparently, the queen wouldn't take no for an answer, and they even ended up arguing about it. In a fit of rage, the queen said, 'How dare you refuse a request from me!' and barred her from the country."

"By the way, they banished me, too, a little while ago."

"I thought as much."

"......"

As I had suspected, she had known exactly what would happen when she sent me on her little errand.

"Afterward, the queen reversed the concepts of ugliness and beauty, then sent the people who she deemed ugly to live outside the gate. And so she lived in peace, happily ever after."

"......"

"How was that?"

"Um, I don't know what to say..." My head had started to hurt.

Let's start by asking the things I want to know.

"So she just exiled everyone to the area beyond the gate, and that was fine? I would expect that some of the people who lived there would have complained."

"Of course, some did. But no one thought to rise up in revolt."

"Oh..."

"The people who were upset with the decision were sent away with large amounts of money. By now they've probably settled somewhere new, don't you think? Though I can't say that was a very clever idea. If they wanted to live in comfort, staying here was the best option. Here you can get basic food and money without even working. It looks like a poor village, but really it's the other side of the gate that's losing out."

"......"

"Thanks to the unfortunate-looking queen imposing her values on everyone, we live peaceful and uneventful lives, and the people over there can live their lives free of disappointment. Holding us in contempt lets them feel better."

"...Ah." *I see.*

So to someone looking over from the other side, everyone over here lives an awful life that leaves them thinking, I never want to be like that. *Each side holds on to the idea that the people beyond the gate are worse off than they are, and that keeps the peace.*

It's clever, yet pathetic, and yet just...ridiculous.

"Well, that concludes my story. What do you think? Did I answer all of your questions?" She held out a hand.

As I placed the book I had bought into her hand, I said, "Yes, mostly. I don't have any more questions." *I'm still stressed out, though.* "By the way, why did you want this book?"

"This is a new release, but they mostly sell them inside the wall. So I got some help from a passing traveler."

"......"

I see. She used me for something very trivial, didn't she?

"And aren't you glad you got to see what it's like over there?"

"True...but I got a little angry when they were so blatantly discriminatory toward me over there."

"Oh... S-sorry about that," she apologized earnestly.

"I don't mind."

Besides, I've got a modest bit of revenge waiting for you every fifty pages in that book.

"As a traveler, what did you think of this land?" she asked me as she was opening the book.

It's very peaceful, but it has a very strange arrangement. Two places in one. If I was going to express my thoughts in one word, it would be—

"Strange. I think it's a strange country."

I felt it could be summed up in that one word.

"I think so, too," she agreed, turning the page.

CHAPTER 12

The Queen of an Empty Country

If you use this map, you oughtta be able to get to the next country. Good luck, missy.

The head of the village I had stayed in the day before had said something like that and pressed a map into my hands, so I had tried my best to follow it.

I spent half a day flying my broom at a low altitude, grazing the ground with the map in one hand. Sure enough, I eventually made it to my destination without incident.

Still, well, how should I put it…?

"……"

This place is a ruin, isn't it? There's nothing here.

Everything was dead. The gate closing off the outside world was left open, and I flew right in without getting off my broom. The interior was in the same state—some houses were roofless, overgrown with moss; some were just skeletal structures; some had been reduced to so much rubble. Rubbish, debris, wreckage everywhere.

There was no sign of life at all, let alone people. Surely, the residents had left long ago. The palace, the symbol of any nation, had retained a comparatively decent exterior, though of course it, too, was abandoned. The outer wall was so full of cracks it seemed like it might crumble at the slightest tap. The wooden door to the palace, however, was unyielding whether I pushed or pulled.

"…Hmm."

I was at a loss. No, really.

Let me see, what should I do? I sat down on the stairs leading to the palace and started to pout, but there was no one here to ask if I was okay, so I just hung my head instead.

Do I spend another half day going back the way I came? Or do I spend a night here? These were the two options open to me. And I didn't want to choose either of them. If I tried to follow the road I had come down, night would fall before I reached a place to stay. Even if I made it back to the village without incident, I didn't know if there was an inn there that would welcome me in. But deciding to forget about the village and sleep here was a troubling proposition, too.

I mean, this place was in ruins.

"...*Sigh.*"

Unfortunately, staying the night in the abandoned palace was the lesser of two evils, and that's what I chose.

When push comes to shove...I really don't want to, but there's no way around it.

I'll stay here.

I stood up. I had to search for a place to sleep.

After surveying the small city from above on my broom, I concluded that the most intact building was the palace. The houses were not an option. Most of them were so crumbled they were useless.

The door to the palace was shut tight, but if you thought about it, the place was already uninhabited.

......Is it okay? ...I can do this, right?

"...Hng." After checking to make sure there was no one around, I used a spell to set the door aflame, reducing it to ash in moments.

"Pardon the intrusion..." I went in.

Despite the cracked exterior, the inside of the palace was still in good condition. It was covered in dust, but I had no objections to sleeping there.

Well then, let's start the search. First up is securing a bedroom.

The empty castle was filled with an eerie atmosphere. It was vaguely disquieting, as if some strange thing might leap out at me at any moment. Feeling a curious chill, I searched for the stairs. I had walked through quite a few palaces as a traveler, so I knew very well that there would be no room to suit my purposes on the first floor. If there was a bedroom, it would be on the second floor. There should also be the bedrooms for the royal family higher up.

I found the stairs within minutes of starting my search and walked up along the dusty carpet.

And then...

"Who are you?"

...I heard a voice.

Reeling as if I had been stabbed in the heart, I looked up and saw a girl standing on the stairs in front of me.

I was about to cry, for more than one reason.

○

"I didn't think anyone was living here."

"I didn't expect anyone to come by."

She had shown me to an elegant bedroom. As far as furnishings went, there was only a desk and a bed, but the room was quite spacious. I guessed that the entire house I had stayed at in the previous village could fit inside this room. *What is this? What's going on? Has she been sleeping here? It's so luxurious.*

"Where did you come from?" She pulled out a chair (a very expensive-looking chair, glittering in pointless gilded splendor) and sat down, then looked at me gently.

"I came from a country far, far away," I said, "I am a traveler."

"May I ask your name?"

"Elaina."

"Is that so? I am Mirarose. Nice to meet you." She smiled.

She had hair as red as blood, and as unkempt as if she'd been zapped with electricity. She wore a tattered dress, too. I was anxious that she might be prone to violence, but she seemed much nicer than I had expected.

"Why are you here, Mirarose?"

"…I don't know."

"Huh? What do you mean, you don't know?"

"I don't know why I'm here." Mirarose's expression twisted. "When I awoke, I was in this ruined place."

"That's…"

It must be amnesia. But how? The country hadn't met its demise yesterday or today. Even by a conservative estimate, it had already been in shambles for at least a month.

I asked her the first thing that came to mind. "Why haven't you left? You could probably live a better life if you moved somewhere else instead of staying here. If you need money, I'm sure you can find some."

If necessity arises, you can always steal valuables from the castle, too.

"……"

She seemed to mull it over for a little while, and then stood up. She pulled a single piece of paper out of a desk drawer and beckoned me over. "Here's the reason why I can't leave."

She showed me the paper. It was covered from top to bottom in messy, meandering handwriting.

It seemed to be a letter. At her urging, I read it.

You, reading this letter, are the queen Mirarose. You know nothing, but I am certain of this.

Why are you here? Why is everything you see outside the window ruined? Why don't you have any memories?

You must be bewildered, faced with all these unknowns, but I want you to be at ease. I will endeavor to explain a bit.

If you are expecting this letter to unravel the great tangle of mysteries you face, you will be disappointed. But at least you can avoid ending your life early with a bad decision. In other words, if you don't wish to die, read on.

By the way, is it currently daytime there, or is it evening?

I'll write with the assumption that it's night. If it happens to be daytime, well, you can just tuck away into a corner of your mind the knowledge that what I am about to tell you will be important later.

I want you to look out the window. You will see a monster on a rampage, I'm sure. That monster is the devil that destroyed this land and the source of your amnesia. It has no name. If we were to borrow from the name of this place and give it a provisional name, we could call it the Javalier.

It rises at sunset and destroys everything it can until sunrise. If you leave the castle to find food, I recommend going during the day. You are safe inside there, as it is the only place the Javalier will not enter.

The goal of the Javalier is to kill everyone in this land. Every night it comes here and goes on a rampage, searching for the last remaining person.

That person, of course, is you.

It hunts for the last queen of an empty country. I'm begging you, please do not leave this place. If you do, the Javalier will follow you wherever you go. This is my one request to you.

I want you to kill the Javalier using your magical powers. You are trapped here until you do, so I don't think you have much choice in the matter. As a witch, you have your magic, so you should be able to take down the Javalier easily. Please kill that monster for our sakes.

For your own, so that you may live.

And for everyone who died in sorrow.

Night fell.

The letter was right; the Javalier was indeed a monster. Its body was huge, about the same height as the decaying buildings, and it was covered in scales as black as midnight.

It had been named the Javalier, but it looked exactly like a dragon if you removed the wings. I can't say for sure, but maybe that resemblance was why it had the terrifying power to breathe fire. It crushed buildings with its big, brawny arms and razed houses to the ground, searching for the last remaining person: Mirarose. It was in an absolute fit of rage.

"Wait, Mirarose, you're a witch?"

"Wait, Elaina, *you're* a witch?"

"Come on, you can tell I'm a witch by looking at me." I was so obviously dressed in a witchy fashion. *Can't you see the brooch?*

"Just joking." Mirarose let out a light chuckle as we watched the monster raging outside.

I followed her gaze. "The person who wrote that letter made a really unreasonable demand, don't you think?"

"They sure did. To fight and win against a monster like that...it's a fool's errand."

"...Come to think of it"—there was something bothering me—"why did they say that only the palace is safe?"

"I have no idea."

Oh yeah, that's right.

"Isn't that letter a little odd? All it really told you was that a monster comes here at night and that you have to kill it, right?"

Although all the little details of Mirarose's current situation were recorded in the letter, the most crucial information was missing.

Why did the Javalier appear, and why was it tearing the place apart? Why was this girl the only person left alive? What was the relationship between the Javalier and her amnesia?

Mysteries, mysteries, and more mysteries. The letter was cleverly cut short, as if to intentionally avoid telling Mirarose the whole story.

Why on earth would someone do that?

"There is a lot I don't know, but I *am* Mirarose, the queen—and my country *was* destroyed by a monster. If those are the facts, then I have an obligation to defeat it... Don't you think?"

"Have you fought that thing?" I pointed to the monster outside the window, and she shook her head.

"Not yet."

"You would never, ever fight a thing like that if you could avoid it, huh?"

"Totally."

"How many days has it been since you first saw the monster, Mirarose?"

"Only seven. Not that much time has passed since I woke up. The place was already destroyed then."

She looked up at the sky. A round moon was glowing pale in the jet-black sky, which shimmered with starlight. *I wonder how she's feeling right now.*

I didn't know. Nor could I know.

"……"

After a brief silence, Mirarose opened her mouth to speak. "Tomorrow night, I'm going to fight that monster."

"Do you have any hope of winning?"

I didn't know whether I would be capable of challenging the Javalier and emerging victorious, myself. It was probably so strong that you could kill it twice and it would still come back to win the fight in the end.

"Of course I do. In the week since I awoke, I've been recalling how to use my magic bit by bit. I think I must have had considerable mastery of it before I lost my memory." She put her hand on her hip.

"Well, do your best. I'll be cheering you on…from a safe distance."

"Oh, you won't help me?"

"What good would that do me?"

"…At least you're honest. I can't really fault you for that."

"Well, thanks for that."

After that, we allowed ourselves to indulge in a friendly chat while watching the massive Javalier continue its rampage. It was a little ridiculous.

For a place to sleep, Mirarose allowed me to use one of the former servants' beds. I was grateful. It was soft and fluffy.

○

Early the following morning, I awoke to a tremendous noise. *Enemy attack! Enemy attack!* my mind shrieked. My heart pounded as if I had just finished running at a full sprint. I jumped up with an ominous feeling in my gut and headed for the first floor, where the noise had originated, gripping my wand.

"Oh, good morning." As I stormed around the first floor with my hackles up, Mirarose greeted me with a cheerful smile. She wore a different dress today, but it was just as tattered as the one yesterday.

Does she only have tattered dresses? Poor thing.

Wait, that's beside the point right now.

"What was that sound just now? An enemy attack?"

"Enemy…?" She tilted her head in confusion. "I was just cooking. Was I really that loud?"

"…? C-cooking?"

I don't suppose there's any chance that what you call cooking is as violent an affair as I'm imagining?

"Yes, it'll be done soon." She nodded and turned to walk away. I followed behind her, and we came to the kitchen.

"Wait in the dining room next door. I'll bring the food in."

"…Um, can I help you?"

"It's fine."

"…Um, thanks."

"Don't worry about it."

"……"

I withdrew, tail between my legs—not that I really had a choice. And so I headed for the dining room and had a seat in one of the chairs at the table. Then it occurred to me. *That was a mistake. I shouldn't have left.*

An incredible din was coming from the kitchen next door, like some kind of high-speed construction. Cracking. Slurping. Chewing. Grinding. Crunching. *I'm begging you, spare my daughter's life—Gyaaah!* Scrubbing. Slapping.

Something like that.

Those were clearly not the sounds of cooking.

To make matters worse, I had heard someone scream. Thanks to Mirarose's fierce cooking (or whatever it was she was actually doing), I had completely lost my appetite.

She brought the food out of the kitchen with a look of satisfaction. I don't have to tell you that I was white as sheet myself.

"Oh my, are you all right? You don't look so well."

"...What on earth were you doing in there?"

"I told you, cooking. Here you go." She placed a plate in front of me. Resting on top of the white plate were two slices of toasted bread. One of the pieces of golden-brown toast was spread with thick red jam. The other piece had a fried egg on top of it.

...Cooking? What on earth were those sounds...?

"Let's eat."

Seated across from me, she pressed both hands together, then crunched into her jam toast.

"...Thanks for the food." I pressed my hands together, too, imitating her.

The more I thought about it, the more I was starting to wonder if I was just losing my mind, so I decided not to sweat the details. Worrying about it was probably a waste of time.

Unlike Mirarose, I started with the fried-egg toast. The flavors of the faintly sweet, delicate wheat and the perfectly fried egg spread through my mouth. It was a common, unsophisticated meal, and that meant it had been a long time since I had eaten anything like this. I smiled despite myself.

To put it simply, it was absolutely delicious.

"I thought we might discuss tonight, while we have the time," Mirarose said.

"Tonight?"

"Yes. I want you to help me with the preparations for my plan."

After nibbling my toast all around the egg yolk, I answered, "You gave me a place to sleep and fed me breakfast; you don't need to ask me to help you."

"Oh, then you'll take down the Javalier?"

"Let's not get carried away."

Why do you have to fight it in the first place? I don't see a problem with just leaving it alone.

Mirarose's expression was gentle, probably because she had already predicted that I would be firm in my refusal. "It was just a joke, so you can set your mind at ease. I must deal with the affairs of my own nation. I'm certain that is what the letter writer would have wished for as well."

"......"

I'm not so sure.

I was silent. Not because I was trying desperately to chew without letting the egg yolk spill out of my mouth. No, really.

"I'm not surprised you feel the way you do, Elaina. It's obvious the letter is not entirely truthful. It would be foolish to believe everything it has to say when it leaves out all the important details."

I was shocked. It was as if she had read my mind.

My words stuck in my throat. Ignoring me, she continued, "However, without any of that information, all I can really do now is fight. Even so...somehow I just can't convince myself that the letter is lying. The writer really hated the Javalier and wanted it dead, and that's why they wrote me that letter. I can just tell."

I pounded on my chest in distress, and Mirarose quietly passed me a cup with water in it. *Ah, how kind.*

"...*Phew!* Thank you." After I took a breath, I said, "No matter what you decide, I'm just a humble traveler, so this isn't really any of my business. However, if you'll allow me to say one thing, if I were in your shoes, I would completely ignore everything that letter has to say."

"Why?" Mirarose smiled. It was not a sneer or an attempt to disguise some other unpleasant emotion; she was simply enjoying our conversation.

What an incredible person. Really.

"Because it's suspicious. That's reason enough. You've lost your memory, you don't know right from left, and yet you're swallowing everything in the letter whole. Of course, it's easy for me to say that. I'm not in your position."

"Well, what would you do if you were me, Elaina?"

"Run. Run away at full tilt and seek asylum in another country," I asserted.

"But the letter said that if I left, the Javalier would come after me."

"That makes it even more suspicious. All it does is tear apart the town; it doesn't have a shred of intelligence. Could it really track you down? Plus, it doesn't make any sense that it can't come into the castle, and the author didn't even sign their name... It's a truly puzzling letter."

"So you don't believe it."

"I don't. Mirarose, have you made up your mind to fight that monster all the same?"

"Of course." She nodded.

In that case, I knew what I had to do.

I took a bite of my jam-covered toast. The odd-tasting jam stuck to the inside of my mouth.

O

The preparations proceeded without delay. However, I did them all myself.

"......"

...I'm exhausted.

Mirarose was elegantly sipping tea and watching me work. "How is it?" she asked in a carefree tone. "Does it seem like you'll finish?"

I turned around, still waving my wand around like mad, and said, "…H-how long do I have to do this until it's finished anyway?"

Peering down into the hole, she answered cheerfully, "Let's see. It looks like you're about halfway through the digging."

"…I'm gonna die." *I'm sure it's just my imagination, but there seems to be an imbalance between the amount of manual labor I'm doing and what I'm getting in return.*

If you're wondering what she was making me do, I was digging a hole. *"I want you to go to the broadest street in town and use magic to dig a hole large enough for the Javalier to completely fit inside."* That was her "preparations."

According to her, the Javalier had no wings, so if it fell into a pit, it should take some time for it to climb back to ground level.

"If we cast magic spells at it nonstop while it's down there, we should be able to bury the Javalier, right?"

That was her plan.

At first glance, one might think this was a reckless plan, but right now, this primitive pitfall trap was our best bet against the mysterious monster. Just one attack should be enough to blast the Javalier apart, so if Mirarose could simply block any sort of counterattack, we could expect the plan to be quite effective.

If the preparations didn't kill me first.

"H-hup…urgggh…"

We had gathered up every single scoop and shovel, and even bucket, in the area, and I was doing my best to operate them all at once using magic. I think I deserved a pat on the back for that. I wanted to be praised for my efforts and hard labor.

Well, I was the Ashen Witch, and I had earned my title with real ability. Of course, I could have done this more efficiently—excavating directly into the ground, for example. However, that would have exhausted an extraordinary amount of magical power. I weighed the alternatives of my own physical labor versus exhausting my magic and chose plain hard work.

And this was the result.

"…Guhaaa…"

And yes, I did regret it.

This is so hard I might actually die.

Eventually, Mirarose started helping, and we made good progress. Even so, it took a good while, and the pit was completed around nightfall. The two of us stood there happily in front of our beautiful hole. After laboring together, I felt a somewhat strange friendship blooming between us. Maybe it was my imagination.

"…It won't be long," Mirarose said. She looked somewhat stiff from nervousness.

"Are you all right?"

"I'm f-f-f-fine. Yes, I'm all right."

Somehow, I'm not convinced. "You're shaking a lot, though."

"I'm t-t-t-trembling with excitement. C-can't you tell?"

"……"

Are you really going to be able to fight like this?

I racked my brain thinking about how to calm her nerves and hit upon the brilliant idea of changing the subject. *I'm a genius.*

"Come to think of it, I forgot to ask you something."

"Oh? What could that be?"

"Why do you wear tattered dresses, Mirarose? Do you not have any nice clothing?" I said.

"Oh, no. It's just that my clothes always get like this when I cook, and changing is a pain, so I just wear them this way."

"What kind of cooking are you doing…?" I was disappointed by the trivial explanation. I was expecting her clothes to be hiding a big secret.

"Anyway, this will serve as my uniform for the battle."

"But now they're tattered *and* muddy."

"Actually, my undergarments are also part of the uniform."

"Are you planning to show them off to the Javalier?"

"It's an attack with sex appeal."

"If only that would work."

As we continued our ridiculous conversation, the smile returned to her face.

Thank goodness. My strategy was a success.

However, just as the relief set in, she said, "Thank you."

"...Huh? For what?" I turned my face away from her. The heat I felt in my cheeks was just from the sunset. Definitely.

"I understand what you're trying to do. You're trying to ease my nerves."

"Hey now, we were just having a chat. I'm sorry if you felt that way. Don't be upset."

"You're ridiculously straightforward, and yet you can't be honest." Mirarose poked me in the side with her wand. It tickled. "I'm fine. I won't die," she said. "Let's meet up again afterward. I'll treat you to my home cooking for dinner."

"That's all right. I'll make dinner tonight," I said. "So don't die, okay?"

"Of course not." As she spoke, Mirarose used magic to hide the surface of the pit. This way, the Javalier should run right into it without knowing any better.

The last rays of the setting sun painted the distant sky red. The horizon split into distinctly red and blue halves, both of which would soon be overtaken by the darkness. And not long after that, the Javalier would come.

"All right, off you go." Mirarose pushed me away.

"See you later," I said, and she smiled gently at me again. And so I turned my back on her and walked off.

O

Hang on—who said I was leaving?

That was a joke. If I left now, it would be all over for my humanity.

Though I think I was being very levelheaded when I turned her down at first.

At the moment, I was inside a house on the other side of the pit, waiting quietly for the right time to strike. The strategy was to make a concentrated attack. To be honest, I hadn't been planning to help if I could avoid it. I mean, the situation didn't have anything to do with me. I had no idea whether it was worth risking my life, or whether there was any real need to defeat the monster.

But my feelings had changed, just a little. I didn't want to let that wonderful girl die. That's why I was going to fight.

And I was going to fight hard enough to survive, of course.

Even now, I couldn't just jump in and offer to help, but I hope it's a forgivable offense.

"……"

Before long, I heard a dreadful roar that sounded as if it had welled up from hell itself. It was very near. When I sneaked a peek outside, I could see black scales slowly passing by.

If it continues on that path, it ought to fall right into the pit.

"…*Phew*," I sighed deeply.

It was strange. Even though I had only just met her yesterday, I really wanted Mirarose to live. When this was over, we would make dinner together, and I would take the opportunity to see her fierce style of cooking. I was really intrigued by it.

As I lost myself in thought, at last the time came, and I heard the monster howling. The sound of its rampage was fainter than before, but the reverberations still reached my hiding place.

I stealthily peeked outside, where Mirarose was fighting an admirable battle. She was mercilessly launching spell after spell against the Javalier as it attempted to crawl up out of the hole. Spears of ice, balls of fire, swords and axes made with magic, blades of wind and lightning bolts, and other spells rained down on the monster.

Eh? Huh? She looks like she might win, I thought for a moment, but my first impression was mistaken. She was definitely doing her best, but Mirarose was struggling.

The Javalier was blowing flames up into the sky, negating Mirarose's spells as it tried to crawl back up out of the hole.

If I'm going out there, now's my chance. If we strike at it together, we should be able to send it back into the hole again. And then bury it there.

I shut my eyes and took another deep breath. I gripped my wand tightly. *Let's do this.*

"Mirarose!" I readied myself and leaped out into the open.

Just as I did, something whizzed by my side with unbelievable speed.

Whoosh. Smearing my face with something as it went, it crashed into the house behind me with a thunderous noise.

I touched my hand to my face and noticed a faint iron smell. This slimy, lukewarm liquid was blood.

...Blood. No way. No, it can't be...

Struggling to keep my pounding heart under control, I turned around.

"......Ah."

There, buried in a mountain of rubble...

...it was...

...the black, dragon-like head of the Javalier. It had been cleanly decapitated, as if with a very sharp blade; fresh blood was pouring from the wound and pooling on the ground beneath it.

Why is the Javalier's head here? Huh? Don't tell me...don't tell me she won without me?

I was standing there, unable to fully grasp the situation, when I heard a voice. "...While I was battling the Javalier, I remembered." Her icy tone sent chills up my spine, and at first I doubted it was Mirarose at all.

But when I turned around, Mirarose was the one standing beside the headless Javalier.

"I remembered all of it, everything, everything, everything. Ah-ha, ah-ha-ha-ha, ha-ha!"

I wondered whether this girl was really the one I knew.

Tearing at her own hair, Mirarose cast more spells. Instantly, the four limbs of the headless Javalier were severed and flew off in different directions. The flying cuts of meat sprayed blood as they went, covering the already destroyed city with gore.

"……"

I shuddered.

She was smiling, bathed in blood. Her expression wasn't the gentle smile she showed me this morning, but something twisted and dark.

"Ah-ha, ah-ha-ha-ha! Ha-ha-ha-ha-ha-ha-ha!"

Words failed me. I could do nothing but stand there in shock.

O

After we returned to the castle, Mirarose told me everything.

It was quite a tale, and she gave me all the details.

Several years ago, she had had a lover.

However, he was a servant, and they had kept their relationship secret from everyone. If her father had found out that she had fallen in love with a boy from a different social class, he would have disowned her. Out of fear, she kept his company in secret, so as not to be discovered.

The two of them had nothing but trust and love for each other.

However, all secrets come to light sooner or later, and theirs was no exception. The fact that she was in love with a servant became a well-known piece of gossip.

Then Mirarose became pregnant with his child. Realizing that it was no longer possible to hide their love, the two of them confessed everything to Mirarose's father, the king.

The king listened silently to their story, nodding seriously several times, and when they finished, he announced, "The servant will be executed."

No one could appease his wrath.

The king carried out the punishment himself. He mounted a horse and dragged the servant around the city behind a carriage, carefully pulled his nails off one by one, smashed his teeth, submerged him in water, gave him just enough food to keep him from starving, held him teetering between life and death for two months, and tortured him in every other way imaginable until the boy went mad, then finally brought his wretched life to an end by burning him at the stake in front of Mirarose and all the citizens.

Then, after he was finished with the servant, it was Mirarose's turn.

As she was his beloved daughter and the country's only witch, the king didn't kill her, but he couldn't forgive her for carrying a servant's child in her belly. The king paid a high sum to a local doctor to secretly terminate her pregnancy. Naturally, the child was never born, no matter how many months she waited.

And so, having lost everything, Mirarose made a vow. A vow to kill everyone.

She carefully developed a plan. The very first thing she did was to block off the castle. For the purpose of her plan, the castle would have to become a reliable safe haven. Since the other people who lived there were getting in the way of her preparations, she locked them all in the basement.

Everyone, that is, except the king.

She threw the king out of the castle and sealed him out. It was a seal so strong that only an individual possessing strong magic powers could break it—which was why I, a witch, had been able to enter.

Next, she had written a letter to her future self—rather, she had the letter written for her. She pulled one of the castle residents from the basement prison and ordered them to do the writing while she stood next to them dictating. If the letter had been in Mirarose's own hand, it could jeopardize the plan.

Then, after concealing the letter she had written in a desk drawer, she looked down from the window of her room at the king, who was trying desperately to get into the castle. The king spotted her, and his ire rose again. He shouted awful things at her: "This is all because you got pregnant with a servant's child" and "You are no longer my daughter!"

She calmly lowered her wand at the clamoring king and cast a spell on him…trading her own memory for the spell's power.

The magical energy born from Mirarose's memories and despair washed over the king and transformed him. He grew extremely large, scales appeared on his skin, and he seemed to lose all of his human intelligence. He became a black dragon.

The king's name had been Javalier. It was no simple coincidence that the monster had the same name. With the creation of the monster that would only be active at night, her plan was complete. Her magic nearly exhausted, she fell into a deep slumber.

The next time Mirarose opened her eyes, she had forgotten everything. However, it had all gone according to plan. At that point, there was nothing to do but walk down the path she had laid out for herself. Mirarose's battle against the black dragon was also part of the plan, as was the fact that during the battle, the memories bound to the monster would return to her.

However, I still had some questions.

Why had she gone out of her way to transfer her memories? Mirarose must have been quite troubled to have woken up with amnesia. Moreover, I wondered if retaining her memories would have made this less unpleasant.

When I asked her, she let out a little laugh. "I gave the king my memories to show him my anguish."

In truth, King Javalier had not lost *all* of his human intelligence when he became a black dragon. Apparently, though his body had been taken over by the transformation, his human consciousness still existed within a corner of the beast's mind. That was Mirarose's plan for him.

She must have wanted to torment the king very badly indeed to go through with such a complicated plot. After becoming a rampaging monster, King Javalier had crushed his subjects with his own hands. With his head full of the memories that Mirarose had forced into him, he had slaughtered the subjects he had once loved, and then...

...And then the rest proceeded neatly according to her plan, and the story came to an end. She had become the queen of an empty country, all by her own doing.

○

The following morning, I left the castle without so much as touching the breakfast that Mirarose had fixed for me.

"You're going already, are you?" she said calmly. She didn't seem particularly saddened by the idea.

"I'm sorry. I am a traveler, after all. I must hurry to the next place."

"Oh, is that so? That's too bad. It was so much fun talking with you."

"......"

"Can't you spend a little more time here?"

"Please, stop."

"I'm only kidding." She smiled, but there was nothing gentle about it anymore. It was twisted and full of darkness. The girl I had come to know was nowhere to be found.

"What will you do now, Mirarose?"

"Let's see, what shall I do...? If I feel up to it, I suppose I could go traveling."

"I don't recommend it."

"You wouldn't mind if I joined you, would you?"

"Really, stop."

"Kidding again. The truth is, I haven't thought of anything yet. For now, I want to savor my vengeance." She rubbed her belly, just like a mother who was nurturing new life.

There was nothing more I could say, so I decided to wrap things up.

"Well, good-bye, then. Take care." I got on my broom as I spoke.

"You too."

I took off into the air and made a beeline through the wind.

She must be waving good-bye. But I don't feel like looking back.

I left that place as fast as I possibly could, speeding past the rubble of her fallen land.

CHAPTER 13

The Start of a Journey

When I was young, I loved books.

I can't even remember when I started reading, but I've been a book-worm for as long as I *can* remember. Whenever I had free time, I would pull a book from the shelf at home and read, and nearly every time my family went out, I would pester my parents for a new one.

Maybe that's why I didn't have many friends my age. I didn't play outside much, choosing instead to spend my time holed up in my room. My parents worried about me, but I had everything I wanted in life. After all, I always had a book by my side.

Among my books, I had a favorite novel series called *The Adventures of Niche*. A short story collection in five volumes, it contained the adventures of a witch named Niche who traveled to various exotic locales across the globe.

The author's name was Niche, same as in the title. But that was simply a pen name; her real name was something completely different. In the afterword to each volume, she wrote, "I penned these novels based on my own experiences."

To young Elaina, a girl who had not taken a single step outside of the Peaceful Country of Robetta, the hero Niche, who wandered from place to place as she pleased and saw the wide, beautiful world, was a shining beacon. I loved those books maybe a little too much and read them all many times. The books started to fall apart.

And eventually, I decided I wanted to be just like Niche.

I want to try traveling like that, too, I began to think.

And so young Elaina made an announcement to her mother. "When I grow up, I'm going to go on an adventure like Niche," I said.

Gently patting my head, my mother answered, "All right, when you grow up." She smiled and added, "But if you want to travel, first you'll have to become a witch like Niche, okay?"

"If I become a witch, I can become a traveler?"

"Yes. That's why you must try your hardest at your magic studies."

"Study hard, become a witch, and then I can travel?"

"Of course."

"Really?"

"Yes, really."

"Really, really?"

"Yes, really, really."

"Yay!"

It all started from such a small thing, but my desire to see the world spurred me on through the years I spent working to become a witch.

I spent almost every day studying alone.

My mother kept me company while I practiced my magic.

My mother was so skilled at magic that you would be surprised to know she had never had any formal training. She was a good teacher, and before I knew it, I was quite good at using magic. So good, in fact, that I was able to become an apprentice witch at the age of fourteen.

It was a long, arduous path, but never once did I think of quitting. I simply continued working hard.

Then I completed my training with Miss Fran and became a full-fledged witch.

O

I believe it happened several days after I returned to my parents' home with the star-shaped brooch on my robe. I was sitting across from them at the table after we had finished breakfast, and I said, "I'm a witch now, so please allow me to travel."

My father lifted his head from his newspaper and frowned. My mother didn't look particularly surprised and calmly sipped her after-breakfast tea.

My father glanced at my mother's reaction, then cleared his throat forcefully, folded his newspaper, and laid it on the edge of the table. "D-don't you think it's best not to rush into anything?" he asked, acting as neutral as possible.

I was a little miffed. "That's not what you said before, is it? Didn't you promise me that when I became a witch I could go traveling?"

"Well, we might have promised that, but…we never thought you'd become a witch so soon…"

"What does that matter? I worked as hard and fast as I could so that I could go and see the world when I finished."

"…Humph."

Defeated, my father slumped back, and after grumbling a bit, clapped a hand on my mother's shoulder. She was still gracefully sipping her tea beside him. "N-now, you say something, too, Mama."

My mother set down her teacup. "Goodness. You're the only one who's against Elaina setting off on her trip, Papa. I think it's just fine for her to go traveling."

"But…"

"And besides, haven't we been telling her this since she was a little girl? We said we would allow her to travel once she became a witch."

"Maybe *you* made that promise—"

"You agreed to it, too. Have you forgotten?"

"But…"

"You agreed, didn't you?"

"……"

My father was silent. Well, more like *silenced*, really.

"Elaina, you're serious about this, right?" my mother asked me.

I nodded. "Of course."

"Then go see the world."

"Okay!"

After a brief pause, my mother said, "However, I want you to make me three promises."

"…Promises?" I tilted my head in confusion.

My mother turned to me and held up three fingers. "Yes. If you can't keep these promises, there's no way I can send you on a journey, witch or no. After all, it's a dangerous world out there."

"…What do I need to promise you?" I sure wasn't giving up now.

"Well, listen up." My mother folded her ring finger. "First, when it seems like you might be heading into a dangerous situation, that you will run away whenever possible. Don't go poking your nose where it doesn't belong. Otherwise, you might end up dead."

"Got it."

That's just common sense. I'd do that even if you didn't make me promise. I'm not ready to die, you know.

My mother continued, folding her middle finger. "Second, never begin to think you are above everyone else; you may be a witch, but you will still be a visitor. You must not get arrogant, and never forget that you are the same as anyone else."

"Okay." Thanks to my experience training under Miss Fran, the weirdly arrogant version of Elaina was already a thing of the past. I didn't think there would be any issue with keeping this promise, either.

"Third…" My mother dropped her loosely folded fist to her side and smiled. "…You must come back. Return, and let us see your smile again."

"……"

"Promise?"

"…Yes." I nodded slowly.

That's when my father started crying. "A-are you really going, Elainaaa…?!"

"Papa, she's made her decision. Let's give her a little push, okay? Besides, we're the ones who promised her that she could go. Parents don't break promises."

"I was sure Papa was going to a minute ago…," I mumbled. Luckily, he didn't seem to hear me.

Wiping away his tears, my father said, "My precious only daughter is already leaving the nest, huh? I can feel a hole opening in my heart already..."

"I mean, I'll come back sooner or later."

"You're going to die of shock when Elaina gets married, aren't you, dear?"

"Stop it! Don't even talk about her getting married; it's too early!" My father started crying again.

......

So that's roughly how it went.

It was officially decided that I would set off on my journey.

○

The following day, I dressed myself in a new outfit.

"Yes, the size is perfect."

My black pointy hat and black robe were hand-me-downs from my mother.

"Isn't it a little too plain?" I did a twirl in front of the mirror.

"Goodness. A plain appearance is perfect for a traveler. Plus, it suits you."

"Thanks."

"You have money?"

"Plenty."

"Don't waste it."

"Of course not."

"And then...ah, that's right. Just in case, take this with you."

"...?"

She plopped a pointy hat down into my hand. It was exactly the same design as the other hat my mother had already put on my head a moment ago. ...*But why?*

"Just in case your first hat blows off in the wind, you can use this one," my mother said to me as I stood there in confusion.

In other words: "A spare?"

"That's right."

Okay, I'll take it.

And then, my preparations complete, I stood in the doorway.

The two of them were standing there when I looked back.

"Safe travels, Elaina." My mother was waving good-bye with a smile on her face.

"Uu, guw…waaahhh…" My father had burst into tears again.

Stroking my father's head, my mother spoke to me with a gentle smile. "Whenever you come back, be sure to tell us all about the Journey of Elaina."

"You can look forward to it while you wait."

"We will. Safe travels."

I tipped my hat, gave them my biggest smile, and said:

"I'm off."

©Azure

CHAPTER 14

Royal Celestelia

As I sailed over the field on my broom, a ripple ran through the flowers to mark my progress. Bathed in sunlight, the blossoms streamed past with a shimmer and a sound like a babbling brook.

I inhaled deeply, filling my lungs with air, and opened my eyes.

On the other side of the field stood a country surrounded by a wall.

Just how massive is this place?

I thought about trying to fly around the outside on my broom, but I doubted I would make it back before sunset, so I gave up on that idea.

More importantly, the gate was right in front of me, so there was no need to go out of my way to fly around. I kept straight on ahead, enjoying the scenery, and landed.

A gate guard came out and quietly bowed to me. "Welcome to our country, Madam Witch. Pardon the intrusion, but may I have your name?"

It was the usual immigration inspection.

"Elaina."

"How long do you intend to stay?"

"About three days, I think."

"What is your witch title?"

"The Ashen Witch."

"…The Ashen Witch?" The guard stared at me.

"Is something wrong?" I probably looked puzzled.

"Ah, no, it's nothing. Pardon me."

The guard looked flustered, but he left me without completely losing his composure.

That seemed to be the end of the questions. I paid one silver for the entry toll and passed through the gate. Behind me, I heard someone say, "Welcome to Royal Celestelia."

○

I was wary because of the country's formal-sounding name, but the city was bustling with energy.

Royal Celestelia was just another strange moniker.

The brick-patterned walkways were filled with people—happy-looking couples holding babies, older children chasing after one another, elderly folks out for a stroll. Everyone was going about their daily lives.

I walked on.

Tall buildings lined both sides of the street, with ropes stretched between them. Clothes were draped over the ropes in the sunlight; someone had put laundry out to dry.

I took a deep breath, and there was a slightly sweet smell. I spotted a flower vase on a windowsill, filled with beautiful multicolored blossoms.

The city before me was so wonderful that it seemed like I might lose track of the time.

I was wandering aimlessly around town when I happened upon a very elegant building. It had a tall clock tower, and the place was so large that I thought it might be a palace. The expansive grounds were enclosed by an iron fence, so I couldn't get close to the building itself.

Gazing at the clock tower, I walked along the fence and discovered the entrance.

Royal Magic Academy

That's what's written on the gate, so I suppose that's what this is. Interesting to find a magic academy here... There had been no such thing in my country. Certainly nothing this fancy.

It was enough to make me jealous of the children who lived here.

...I'm a little curious about the inside. Is it all right to go in? Should I go in?

Well, I'm going in anyway.

I stepped onto the grounds.

"Hey, you. What're you doing?"

I hadn't made it far when someone grabbed me firmly by the shoulder.

"It's prohibited for unauthorized persons to enter. It's fine to look, but I'm going to have to ask that you stay outside."

When I turned around, there was a brawny man standing there. His clothing was stretched tight over bulging muscles. He seemed to be the gatekeeper.

"......"

"...Oh." He looked down at my chest, and his attitude changed completely. "Beg your pardon. I didn't realize you were a witch... Please excuse my rudeness."

"No problem." I shook off his hand and walked toward the school again.

"Terribly sorry, but please don't go in there." I was stopped again.

"Ah, so it's prohibited?"

"Yes."

"Even for witches?"

"My orders are that anyone from outside is absolutely forbidden."

"Who gave you those orders?"

"The great witch who runs this Academy."

"...Huh."

"She doesn't want the secrets of the Academy's curriculum to escape. She couldn't bear to have our methods stolen by an imitator."

"Well then, how about closing the front gate?"

"We can't do that. It's almost time for the great witch to arrive."

"...Huh." I left reluctantly.

Too bad.

*　　*　　*

It's still too early to find an inn for the night, hmm?

I continued walking aimlessly. It was fun just wandering around this country.

"......"

I looked up and saw a broom flying above the houses, but it didn't look like it was just drifting around. The man atop it was zigzagging over the houses, dropping things as he went. When I saw someone come out on their veranda and open it, I realized the man was delivering newspapers.

I walked down the main street and found a street packed with stalls on either side: fruit stands, grocers, butchers, and more. There was also a bread stall, with a sign that said FRESH BAKED!

No bigger lie than that, huh? I bet it's all stale.

"Excuse me. I'll have one loaf of bread, please."

The friendly-looking woman behind the counter grinned at me. "That'll be one copper."

I took a copper coin out of my wallet and handed it to her.

The woman grabbed my loaf and thrust it into a bag...with her bare hand.

"Here you go. Thanks."

"Yeah...thanks."

I took it and wandered the shopping district munching on bread. The long, thin loaf was clearly not freshly baked, as it was stiff and hard. I continued on, grappling with it, and eventually left the commercial area.

Then I saw another mage. This man had a large bundle tied to his broom, and he was speaking with the proprietor of a café.

"Deliver this to the home of Miss Amana, who lives on the west side of town. Carry it carefully! It's got her lunch inside, okay?"

"Roger!"

"Oh, I'm not so sure about this..."

Giving the café owner a sidelong glance, the man slowly rose up on his broom and flew off somewhere.

So they're doing deliveries by broom, I see. This country must have a lot of mages for some reason.

I guessed it was because they had a school teaching magic.

Mages weren't just handling newspapers and package deliveries, either; some were carrying people, too, in buggies attached to their brooms. Of course, it wasn't practical for one person to carry such a heavy load alone, so they worked in teams of two. One person appeared to be in charge of operating the broom, while the other seemed to be lightening the buggy itself using magic.

There were mages not only in the sky, but on the ground as well. Some were demonstrating magic on the shoulder of the main street, to the delight of the people around them. They were creating puppets with magic and putting on a play.

Some were singing as they livened up the place with magic effects (producing snow and the like), keeping the crowds excited.

All of the mages were working energetically.

By the way, there was something weighing on my mind a bit.

I think it's great that the mages here can enjoy their lives, but isn't it taxing?

So I decided to ask. Asking someone is the quickest way to find out something you don't know, right?

"Excuse me." I spoke to a mage girl who was sitting on a bench reading a book (she had neither a brooch nor a corsage, so she was probably a novice). I was in a plaza I had found by coincidence.

"Yes? What is it?" She turned toward me with a soft expression.

"I am a traveler, and there's something that's been bothering me. If it's all right, could I ask you about it?"

"My, what a cute traveler you are." She giggled. "All right, what is it? I'll tell you if I know."

I paused for a moment, then said, "Isn't it difficult for the mages in this country to fly?"

She tilted her head in confusion. "Difficult to fly…? No, not really."

"Even with those?" I pointed to the ropes strung between the tall buildings and the clothing hung from them.

Her gaze followed my finger, and she let out a knowing sound. "Ah… Those were put up on purpose."

"On purpose?"

"Yes. This country has many mages, right? That's why we make it so difficult to fly around."

"…?" I didn't know what she meant.

"Oh my. Was that not enough to explain?"

"Yes, if you could walk me through the logic…"

She laid her book to the side. "The farther you get from the ground on your broom, the more exhausting flying becomes, right? So everyone wants to fly as low as possible."

"Right," I agreed.

"But if everyone flew low to the ground, it would get congested. And someone might even crash into a house trying to avoid the other people passing by. That's a real risk when there are so many mages."

Ah, I see now. "So to keep people from flying in between the houses, you've put up ropes and clothing to block the way?"

She said with a smile, "Exactly. In this country, we believe mages must be considerate of those who cannot use magic."

"…And none of the mages have a problem with that?"

"Can't you tell just by looking at how things are here?"

O

I pulled my broom out and flew up into the sky. I wasn't going anywhere in particular. I just wanted to see the place from above.

"…Wow." The view from the air was totally different from the view from the ground. The multicolored roofs were lined up at about the same height in a pattern of red and blue, aqua and yellow. The wind blowing past me was pleasant, and I thought about how great it would feel to lie down on one of those roofs and gaze up at the sky.

It would be a good idea to search for tonight's inn from up here, too.

I flew around aimlessly, nodding greetings to the mages I passed and waving back to the children who waved at me from the insides of buggies.

I was passing the time pleasantly enough when a thought came to me. *This reminds me, in one of the countries I visited earlier, didn't a girl suddenly crash into me as I was flying through the air? I wonder what she's doing right now? Maybe she's in training to become a witch back in her hometown.*

"......"

I stopped my broom in midair, yanking the handle up sharply. I had gotten sentimental remembering Saya... No, that wasn't the reason, of course. In fact, the two people who had pulled up in front of me had reminded me of Saya.

"Um, can I help you?"

A boy and girl were blocking my way, apparently on purpose. They wore black cloaks, white dress shirts with red ties, and either black pants or a skirt. No brooches, meaning they were both novices.

"Good day. You are the Ashen Witch, I presume," said the boy.

"Uh, w-we're students at the Royal Magic Academy," said the girl.

The Royal Magic Academy. *Interesting. They're from the school that wouldn't let me in?*

"Do you need something from me?"

"Um... Could we ask you to please come with us, without asking any questions?" The girl's voice was very timid for such a bold request.

This is about as suspicious as it gets. "Why?"

"Oh, I said don't ask any questions..."

"Absolutely not," I answered right away.

"Huh?! Why not?!" the boy was overly surprised.

"Something feels wrong about it, so I'm not going."

I may have revealed my identity, but why do I suddenly have to go with you? And without asking any questions? That's doubly suspicious, isn't it? Forget it.

"Um, but…"

"First, let me hear your reasons. Then I'll decide whether or not I'll go with you," I said firmly to the very shy girl.

"That's…not possible."

"Well then, I can't possibly go with you."

The boy interjected from beside me, "Oh, come on! We're begging you, Ashen Witch! Come with us and please don't ask why!"

"I told you—if you won't tell me why, then I can't go. You're awfully persistent."

……

I could see that this was going nowhere. If we continued the conversation in this vein, we would simply keep talking past one another.

Time to run away?

Yes, I do believe so.

I abruptly wheeled my broom around. "Oh, I'm sorry. I just remembered I have something very urgent to take care of," I lied. And then I flew away from them.

"…Huh?!"

Well, I tried to, but my way was blocked again by mages. There were a number of boy-girl pairs dressed exactly the same as the first one.

Oh, what do we have here? Things are getting stranger and stranger. Looking left and right, I could see quite a few pairs of students in the same outfits closing in on me, one after another. Suddenly, I was completely surrounded by a mysterious group of about twenty students.

"Hey, you guys. Let's gang up on her."

"Yeah."

"If we all work together, we can catch her, probably."

"Okay."

"Got it."

"Don't hog all the glory."

"Same to you."

The students were swaying back and forth. I had absolutely no idea what was going on, but I knew one thing for certain. If I stayed here, they'd catch me. And I didn't know what might happen if I got caught.

"......"

I slowly tilted my broom downward, and then...

"Ey!" I struck the broom and took off with a burst of speed. I held on to my pointy hat with one hand so it wouldn't go flying off as I blasted through the sky over the city at full tilt.

In other words, I made a break for it.

When I looked back, I could see the students coming after me, shouting something or other. And so began an intense chase, for reasons I did not entirely understand.

But to no one's surprise, a full witch had an overwhelming advantage over a bunch of novices.

"......"

They pursued me tenaciously, but I could tell that I was slowly pulling away from them. It was only a matter of time before I shook them off completely. But even if I could shake them, they would have a bird's-eye view of my movements against the background. No matter where I fled, they would spot me again immediately.

Well, what should I do? How about this?

"...Okay." I dropped my speed, turned to the side, and flew just below the rooftops. I could see the ropes strung between the houses, and the clothing hanging from them flapped in the breeze as I flew past.

At this height, the roofs made me harder to see from far away. *If they lose sight of me once, it should be hard for them to find me again.*

When I looked back, there were still several students chasing me persistently. *There were about twenty of them before, so maybe the other students gave up?*

But when I looked forward again, I realized that was not the case. Several students were trying to head me off.

"…Ah!"

They had separated and anticipated my movements. They had the home territory advantage. No question about it.

I turned my broom to the left, speeding down a back alley.

If this is how it's going to be, let's really *make our escape!*

I flew onward a little, and the exit came into view.

However…

"Ah, I found her!" A girl pulled into view, blocking the exit, and stretched a hand out toward me.

They predicted my course again. But if they're this good…

"Just cooperate and let us catch you— Huh?"

Just as the girl got within about one broom-length of me, I jumped into the air. After it passed directly under the dumbfounded novice, I summoned my broom back to me and flew off.

It was a midair breakaway move. On top of being useful against surprise attacks, it looks kind of cool, so I like to whip it out from time to time.

Even after I lost the girl, my path was still blocked, and my pursuers were closing in from front and back. I had thought that flying low would hide me, but they had known my position exactly.

Well, in that case… I flew high up into the sky this time.

"……"

After achieving a certain height, I looked down on the city. The students had noticed my ascent, and now they were coming out from between houses and above the roads to assemble and come after me again. They were slowing down; I think they were getting tired.

I continued to wait high in the sky until they gave chase.

Finally, one male student flew at me from directly beside me, yelling, "Graaaaaahhh!"

I easily moved my broom and dodged him.

"Aaaaaaaaahhh!" With another weird-sounding yell, he flew right past me.

As if that was some sort of signal, the students attacked all at once from every direction. They numbered about…well, I stopped counting after ten. All of the ones who had initially surrounded me were there, probably.

They seemed to have lost the capacity for speech, as what came from their mouths was mostly weird screams.

"Gaaahhh!" "Nyaaahhh!" "Oraaahhh!" "Hyaaahhh!" "Shraaahhh!" "Damnyaaaaa!"

And so on.

I calmly continued to evade my pursuers—left, right, up, down, and sometimes around in circles, dodging, dodging, dodging.

They hadn't started actually attacking me yet, so I also had not pulled out my wand, and I devoted my energy to simply keeping away from them on my broom.

"Gyaaahhh!" "Ahhhhhh…" "Ah…" "Wha…?" "Hah…" "Eeeeeek…" "N-no good…"

I don't really remember how long we kept this up. Before I knew it, the students were flying sluggishly, and then finally, no one was coming at me anymore.

Seems like they've had enough.

They all flew together into a huddle.

"I-impossible…," someone among them panted.

"I-I'm gonna die…" Someone else was white as a sheet.

"What exactly is your objective?" I demanded calmly. "What business do you have with me?"

But there was no answer except for heaving breaths.

"You ought to understand by now that you can't catch me even if you all gang up on me. Give up," I ventured, but I wasn't surprised when no one spoke back to me. Unbothered, I continued, "Well then, who on earth—?" *Asked you to do this?* I swallowed the words that had been about to come out of my mouth.

I couldn't speak anymore.

A witch had arrived.

One of the students followed my gaze and murmured, "Oh, it's Miss…" As soon as they heard that, the other students hurried to straighten their uniforms and fix their hair.

The woman pulled up her broom close to the winded students, wearing a truly radiant smile, and said, "Everyone, good work. How was it? You tried as hard as you could to catch a witch, but you didn't stand a chance, did you? This is the gap in ability between a witch and a student. It has nothing to do with age. It's because the Ashen Witch has genuine power, and you can't compare."

She had hair as black as midnight, a robe and pointy hat in the same shade, and a star-shaped brooch on her breast. She smiled at me, exactly the same as she was three years ago.

This was their teacher.

"It's been a while, Elaina."

Miss Fran.

○

"I'm sorry, Elaina. I'll explain everything. But first, would you please come with us to the Academy?" Miss Fran spoke apologetically, while leading me and the students to the Royal Magic Academy. There was no way to turn down her request. After all, I had so many things I wanted to tell her.

The cluster of twenty young mages flying together must have looked like a flock of migrating birds.

I stared hard at Miss Fran's back, thinking to myself. *She really hasn't changed at all from back then, huh?* I mused. *I wonder how old she is now?*

Before I knew it, we had arrived at the Academy.

Landing her broom on the school grounds, Miss Fran said, "Everyone, this concludes today's extracurricular activities. Good work. Be ready to present your thoughts tomorrow morning."

After replying with hollow-sounding *Yes, ma'am*s and *Thank you*s, the students scattered. They were clearly exhausted; some of them wobbled unsteadily through the air, while others gave up on flying entirely and walked home.

Watching them go, Miss Fran smiled. "My, my. Do you think we went too hard on them, Elaina?"

"And that's my fault?"

"And mine."

"…So you're teaching at this school, too, Miss Fran?"

"Yes. Just before I was asked to take you on for training, the king invited me here."

"……" I had never heard about this. "You mean you were away from the school for a whole year? You're lucky you didn't get fired."

"Yes. Well, I'm not ordinarily in charge of any classes, you see. My specialty is mentoring other teachers, and sometimes I take on extracurricular lessons for those interested, like you saw today. Moreover"— Miss Fran looked at me—"the other teachers were very understanding when I told them I had been teaching you magic," she added.

What does that mean?

"Teaching me?"

"Yes. If my pupil had been anyone else, I probably would have lost my job."

"I didn't think I was that important."

"I wonder," she said, smiling as always. And then she added, "Well, come inside. There's so much I want to discuss with you." She pointed to the school building behind us.

I felt the same way.

The interior of the school building was very plain.

Desks and chairs formed a neat array in a square classroom with a large blackboard at the front. Not a single decoration adorned the walls.

Similar classrooms were lined up along one side of the hallway. Opposite them were windows looking out on the spacious grounds of the school.

"Originally, this school was a place for teaching ordinary subjects," she said. "But when a new one was built, this one became unnecessary. We got them to let us use it as a school for teaching magic, as well as more mundane subjects."

"So the students who were trying to catch me…they go to school here, right?"

She nodded. "Yes. As part of my extracurricular course, I instructed them to either bring you to me without telling you why, or drag you here by force."

"…Why?"

"Can you not figure it out on your own?"

"I don't know."

She was silent for a bit. Then Miss Fran clapped a hand on my shoulder.

"Because I wanted to see you," she said in a very small voice, almost a whisper.

"……"

Complicated emotions swirled inside me. *This woman is cunning*, I thought. *She knows I can't stay angry if she says something like that.* Instead, I changed the subject.

"How did you know that I had come to this city?"

"Because you tried to waltz into the school without permission."

"…Ah."

The large gate was visible outside the window. Of course, I had been stopped by the burly guard near there. Miss Fran followed my gaze and nodded. "That's right. I was informed by the gate guard when I came to school. He said, 'A young witch with ashen hair was trying to get in. I think she might be a spy for another country.'"

"A spy…" *He really jumped to conclusions, huh…?*

"When he described you, I thought, 'Oh, that must be Elaina.' I went straight to the guard at the city gate and confirmed that you had indeed come here."

We reached the end of the corridor. Miss Fran turned the corner and went up the stairs, and I followed her.

"Your name was in the immigration records. You arrived this morning, didn't you?"

"Yes." I nodded.

"'...My apprentice is visiting,' I thought, and I just couldn't contain myself. I decided to search for you...using my students."

"......"

"When I got back to school, I was just in time for the extra class I hold with my highest-performing students. So I gave them a task."

We finished ascending the stairs, and a single door appeared before us. Miss Fran put her hand on the knob and opened it with a loud, unpleasant creak. Perhaps the door fitting was poor.

"'There is a girl in this country called the Ashen Witch,' I told them. 'Bring that witch here without letting her know why.' If they had, by some miracle, been able to force you to come with them, I was thinking about giving them extra credit."

"Why did you take such a roundabout approach...?" *You could have just searched for me normally.*

Miss Fran snorted. "Don't you think it would be nearly impossible for me to search this huge country all by myself?" She leaned back against the door. "Well, go ahead," she prompted me.

I walked past her and went inside. Inside was a room that looked like a combination study and reception room. In the center was a pair of sofas facing each other over a table, and a desk piled with a mess of papers and books stood against the far wall.

I heard another ear-splitting creak as the door closed behind me.

"What's wrong? Have a seat." Miss Fran walked by me and sat on one of the sofas.

"Ah, okay." I sat down on the other, facing my former teacher. The couch was soft and fluffy.

"I knew you had become a traveler, but I was really surprised to learn that you had come to this country, you know?"

...? Huh?

"You knew that?"

"Yes. I knew."

"I don't think I ever talked to you about traveling, Miss Fran."

After all, it had been several years since I had seen her. The only people who knew about my journey lived in the Peaceful Country of Robetta, like my parents. It was awfully strange that Miss Fran would know.

My former teacher must have seen my confusion. "Elaina, do you still remember what I said to you when you finished your training?"

"Good-bye, Elaina. I'll come see you again someday. Please look forward to it and wait for me." I mean, yeah, she did say that, but...

Miss Fran smiled impishly. "I had some business there, so the year after your training I went to Robetta again. While I was there, your mother told me that you had gone traveling."

"You saw my mother?"

"Yes. She was quite worried about you. If you're ever close to home, be sure to pay her a visit."

"I'm planning to."

Though I've come very far, so I suspect it'll be a while before I can go see her again.

"That's good." After pausing for a moment, Miss Fran asked, "Come to think of it, why did you want to become a traveler, Elaina? Was it your mother's influence?"

...? Why is my mother part of this conversation? My head tilted in confusion.

"Uh, no it wasn't... When I was little, I read a book series called *The Adventures of Niche*. That's what had the biggest influence on me."

"......Oh my." Miss Fran's eyebrows rose just a bit. "Hmm...I see." She seemed to be mulling over that information. It was a strange reaction.

©Azure

"Um, what is it?"

Miss Fran shook her head at my question. "No, it's nothing. So *The Adventures of Niche*, was it? You've got good taste. I like those books, too."

"Oh-ho-ho. I've read them so many times, I can recite every story from all five volumes from memory," I boasted.

"My, my. In that case, what's your favorite story? I quite like the last one, 'Fuura the Apprentice Witch.'"

"…! That's my favorite, too!"

If I remember correctly…in that story, Niche the witch visits a certain country, takes on an apprentice, a girl named Fuura, and helps train her to become a witch. At the end of the story, Niche abandons the life of a witch and goes to live in the countryside as a normal woman. Then Fuura becomes a witch herself and begins a new series of travels.

"By the way, the apprentice witch Fuura and I are a lot alike." Miss Fran said something strange.

"What are you saying?"

"Let's see—what am I saying?" Miss Fran laughed. "*The Adventures of Niche* is a famous work. It's very popular even in this country."

"But it's a very old story, isn't it?"

"Good books stand the test of time."

"…I suppose that's right." Nothing sparks more joy for longstanding fans.

If I wanted to, I could probably spend part of my travels going around and directly promoting *The Adventures of Niche*… Though my budget constraints would likely cause setbacks in the end.

"Anyway," Miss Fran interrupted my thoughts. "When are you planning to leave, Elaina?"

"…I was thinking the day after tomorrow."

"The day after tomorrow?"

"Yes."

I can't stay too long. Especially since Miss Fran is here.

"What are your plans for tomorrow? Is there anything you have to get done?"

"Tomorrow? No, not really..."

"So you're free?" Miss Fran asked enthusiastically.

What is going on?

Still a little confused, I answered, "Well, I am free...but..." It wasn't like I had nothing to do, but my plans were just sightseeing. Technically, I did have the time.

"That's great." Miss Fran smiled.

"What is?"

"It's just that tomorrow, there's something that I want you to help me with."

"Oh. Sure, I don't mind—what can I do?"

"I want you to help me teach."

"......"

That's a little suspicious...

"I want you to help me teach."

Why did she say it twice?

Very suspicious...

After that, we talked about all sorts of things. I got so engrossed in the conversation, I completely forgot about the time. We talked about all the different people I had met on my travels, I told her about the places I had visited, and she told me about people from elsewhere, whose names I didn't know. The conversation never stopped for a moment.

I wished that time could stand still, but time flies when you're having fun. Before I realized it, the world outside was dark.

"Oh my, it's so late already. Shall we stop here for today and go home?"

I wanted to talk more, though.

As we left the school building, Miss Fran invited me to stay at her house, but I declined. The more she took care of me, the harder it would be to get back to my travels. Parting would become that much more painful.

I walked around searching for an inn in the darkness. During my search, the window of a house caught my eye. Illuminated by the moonlight, the window cast a clear reflection, like a mirror.

I was positively beaming.

○

Morning came.

After waking up in the inn I had found after a lengthy search the night prior, I quickly changed into witchy clothes and set out.

Outside, I mounted my broom and rose up into the sky, headed of course for the Royal Magic Academy. I flew on, exchanging simple greetings with the young men who had been flying around dropping newspapers on houses all morning, as well as the courier pairs who had replaced horses and carts. I had been a little sleepy still, but the chilly early-morning breeze ensured I was wide-awake.

With the large tower to serve as my landmark, I was able to reach my destination quickly, without getting lost. From my bird's-eye view, I could see a bunch of people around the campus. Those were the students.

There were about twenty, the same number of people who'd chased after me the previous afternoon. Miss Fran was there among them.

I brought my broom down next to her and stood beside her. I could feel solid ground under both feet.

"Oh, good morning. You're quite early. I don't believe I gave you a specific time." Miss Fran smiled at me.

"That's *why* I came early."

"Oh my. You aren't upset with me, are you?"

"Oh, no. I just want you to praise me."

"Excellent. Great job."

"Thanks."

"Well, in that case, it seems we can get started earlier than planned."

And then she clapped her hands twice. *Clap, clap.*

When she did, the students hurriedly stopped their drills and gathered around. In fact, it might be better to say they sprinted over with all their might. I also saw some students dump the water they had been using in their practice onto the ground in their hurry.

Turning to the assembled students, Miss Fran introduced me. "Everyone, this is Elaina, the Ashen Witch. You met her yesterday, too, so you know that already, right?"

I gave a quick bow. "Ah, hello."

"Today I'd like to have her conduct a special seminar. She may not be much older than you students, but she is a splendid witch. Don't underestimate her." Then, after all the students nodded in agreement several times, Miss Fran asked them, "Do you have any questions for her?"

A smart-looking, eloquent young man immediately raised his hand. "Me, meee! Do you have a boyfriend? Do you?"

Oops, my mistake. It was a dumb-looking, crude young boy.

"I do not. I'm a traveler, after all."

"Only questions related to magic," Miss Fran cut him off flatly. "Anyone else?"

The next student to raise her hand was a timid-looking girl. I thought she might have been one of the two who had first approached me. She looked at me nervously and asked, "Um… What kind of magic is your specialty…?"

I was relieved to have a normal question. "I don't really have a specialty. I can perform attack spells, manipulation spells, and transformations of all kinds."

"Any other questions?"

Someone put a hand up. "Out of all the places you've visited so far, which one is your favorite?"

"This one."

"Oh my. Do I smell flattery?" Miss Fran chimed in.

More hands went up, one after another. There was no end in sight.

"What made you want to become a witch?"

"I read a book called *The Adventures of Niche*… That's my favorite reason anyway."

"What country are you from, Elaina?"

"The Peaceful Country of Robetta—it's very, very far away."

"Tell me the secret to doing magic!"

"It's just hard work."

"Is it fun being a traveler?"

"Yes. Very fun."

"Me, meee! How about your underwear? What color are they—?"

Miss Fran pinched the rude, dumb-looking boy to within an inch of his life, and as soon as that was done, the Q&A period came to an end.

The morning's extracurricular lesson proceeded without incident.

However, since I was completely unsure about how best to instruct the students, I convinced Miss Fran to let me observe for a while from a distance and see how she taught them.

"Oh my. The flow of your magic is all out of whack. Work on calming your mind and stabilizing your energy."

"You're sending out too much magical energy. Hold back a bit more."

"Hey! Don't make the water into swords. Stop playing around."

…In this vein, she walked around to each and every student, giving very proper guidance as she went.

Hmm, hmm, I see. All right then, let me try to imitate her. I wandered around among the students at an unhurried pace.

They seemed to be in the middle of a series of drills for handling magic. As before, the students were making water inside vases move. It was a basic drill, but the first step to achieving a high level of skill in magic is being able to move things the way you want to.

I was walking around casually when a male student asked, "Uh, Miss Elaina? My water ball won't stay smooth. What should I do?" The water at the end of his wand was indeed floating in the air, but it was bubbling like it was moments away from boiling.

I see, I see.

"You're putting way too much energy into it. Ease up a little bit."

"Okay!"

Immediately, a puddle of water formed at the boy's feet with a *splash*.

"...I lost control of it."

"You eased up too much."

Too bad, I thought, looking at him with pity. He seemed very disappointed.

Behind me, I heard a small voice, lacking confidence. "Uh, um..."

When I turned around, there was the timid girl.

"What is it?" I tilted my head a little bit.

"Um, yes... Um, there's something I'd like you to teach me..."

"Of course. What is it?"

After a short pause, she answered, staring at the ground. "Um, no matter what I do, I can't really control the water... I can just barely lift it up... What should I do?"

Mm-hmm.

"Let me see you try."

"Huh? Um, okay..."

She gripped her wand in both hands, faced the vase full of water, and projected her magical energy. The vase began to move about ten seconds later.

First the whole vase lifted off the ground, then, as if she had remembered what the actual task was, the water rose into the air out of it. Then, as it reached the height of the girl's face, the sphere of water immediately crashed back to the ground.

"Oh my."

"...What should I do?" Her eyes were filling with tears. She looked like she was taking the situation awfully seriously.

"Looks like you don't quite have the hang of it yet. I think that at first, you should spend more time practicing getting the water out of the vase."

"O-okay…"

"After you get the water out of the vase, put it back right away, then take it out again. As you practice that over and over, I think you'll get quite used to it. Don't rush things and find your own way of working. That's the shortest way to success. Do your best, okay?"

"…Y-yes, ma'am!"

That was the best advice I could give. After watching her run off to go scoop water, I started walking around again. As I did, I heard a voice call me from behind.

"Oh, ohhh! Look at me, Miss Elaina! Isn't this cool?" That stupid-looking, rude boy was wearing a crown he had made out of water. I ignored him.

The students were very enthusiastic (all except one) and came up to me to ask my advice themselves. Of course, we were close in age, so it may have been easy for them to ask me questions.

It didn't feel half-bad.

The drills continued until Miss Fran clapped her hands twice again.

As soon as the morning's extracurricular lesson had concluded, Miss Fran's work for the day was also over, apparently.

Based on what had happened the previous day, I would have thought she also had an extracurricular lesson in the evening, but according to her, "If we have it in the morning, we don't have it in the evening. If we don't have it in the morning, we have it in the evening. Basically, it was a once-per-day extracurricular lesson.

"Why do you only do it once?" I asked.

She answered, "Exhaustion, of course."

"You're concerned that doing it twice in one day would exhaust the students?" *I see, I see.*

"No, we don't do it more than once because *I'll* get tired."

"……"

I had no name for the emotion I was feeling.

○

After the extracurricular lesson was over, I followed Miss Fran out of the school building. We flew leisurely through the sky, headed for higher ground. Eventually, Miss Fran landed her broom.

I did the same, and the tender grass swished quietly. The light green of a wide meadow stretched out around us, drawing a gentle arc against the sky. On the other side of a simple wooden fence was the city and its multicolored houses. The trees near us fluttered in the wind, sending leaves floating off into the distance. Beyond the trees stood the school building with its oversize tower, which I had been using as a landmark. There were clouds floating across the clear blue sky, smooth and white.

"Isn't it beautiful? This is a place very dear to my heart," Miss Fran said.

"Yes, I can see why."

"I'm glad you like it." Miss Fran's black hair fluttered softly in the gentle breeze. With a smile, she said, "I wanted you to see it once, before you left the country. I love this view."

Her smile was contagious, and I felt the corners of my mouth tugging upward. "Thank you."

"Don't mention it. So you're leaving tomorrow morning?"

"Yes. I can't stay too long."

"That's too bad… My students really seem fond of you."

"That's just because they're not used to seeing a young witch." *Not to mention a young traveler.*

"Even so, it's wonderful that they took a liking to you. My students often seem to avoid me."

"……"

They don't avoid you; you just don't understand the sense of distance your elusive nature creates. I won't say that, though. I can't say that.

"What is it?"

"...No, nothing."

As if to escape Miss Fran's gaze, I turned my eyes to the school in the distance. "Anyway, you're teaching magic at the Academy, right?"

"Yes."

"What do the students do when they graduate?"

"Usually they work here in the country. For example, delivering packages, or flying people around. If you did any sightseeing here, you must have seen quite a few mages en route above the rooftops, yes?"

I see.

"Were the people putting on magic demonstrations in town Academy graduates, too?" I remembered the street shows, people singing and using magic to operate puppets and create special effects. I wondered if all the mages I had seen in town had in fact studied at the Royal Magic Academy.

Miss Fran nodded. "Yes, well, those people are pursuing their hobbies. Those aren't real jobs."

"Hobbies, huh...? But they get money for it, right?"

"Well, I suppose they do, but I doubt it's very much. Those people aren't performing magic because they want money."

"Then why?"

"It's because they love it," Miss Fran said flatly. "You're traveling because you love to, right, Elaina? It's the same thing. They're doing it because they like to make people happy."

"......"

Not for the money, for themselves, or for someone else. Because they like it.

Ever since I'd stepped across the border of this country, the thought had crossed my mind more than a few times that this was a wonderful place. The cityscape was lovely, and the scenery was lush. People spent their days with smiles on their faces. My heart felt a little tug whenever I saw those happy locals. Perhaps that was because my time in this country of Royal Celestelia had, in some way, reflected my travels themselves.

"Come to think of it, what is something that you love, Elaina?" Miss Fran suddenly asked me.

"Traveling, of course," I answered.

"Besides that."

"……"

If not travel, then what? Well, I suppose the thing that inspired my journey.

"Books, I guess."

"Books…" Miss Fran was silent for a brief moment, then asked again, "Besides books?" She was as frank as ever.

"Um, what is this? Why are you asking?"

"Oh, I'm just a little curious."

"Are you getting me a farewell gift or something?" I asked jokingly.

"Yes, well," she quickly assented, putting me in a tough position.

Oh no. What have I done?

"…Uh, no, that's all right, I don't need a farewell gift. Just your well wishes are plenty."

"Now, now, don't say that. Tell me, what do you like? Perhaps flowers or something?"

"You're already leading me to an answer."

"How about it? Flowers. Ah, and butterflies, that would be good."

"Those are things that *you* like, Miss Fran."

"I like them, so my apprentice must like them, too, right?"

"Your logic makes no sense."

"You don't like butterflies?"

"They're fine."

"I see. You like them just fine."

"I don't hate them, but I don't like them, either."

"How about flowers?"

"And now we're back back to flowers."

"Well? How about them?"

"I mean, I like them…"

"Great."

"What's great?"

"That's for me to know," Miss Fran said with her usual smile. Despite asking me all kinds of random questions, she wouldn't answer any of mine.

Even after living together for an entire year, even after meeting again after all this time, she was the same old Miss Fran. I still couldn't tell just what kind of person she was. But I'm not sure that she really knew, either. I was used to it.

"What is it? Are you planning something?" I knew exactly what she was going to say, but I asked anyway.

And Miss Fran answered just as I expected, winking mischievously. "I'm looking forward to tomorrow."

Let me see, how should I put this…

"I'm leaving this country tomorrow morning, so…"

"Yes, and I'm looking forward to seeing you right before you leave. Let's meet in front of the gate tomorrow morning."

○

Time passed, and morning came.

Strolling leisurely down the main street of the city, I headed for the gate along the same path I had followed the previous day. I walked through the shopping street, gazing at all the mages flying through the air. I passed under the ropes strung between the buildings like so many arches. I could smell the sweet scent of a flowers blooming somewhere.

I walked on—and I didn't really want to leave.

"……"

Soon I arrived at the gate.

The guard bowed when he noticed me. I lowered my head, too, a little late.

If I continued just a bit farther, I would leave the country. However, looking around, I couldn't see Miss Fran anywhere.

...We didn't specify a time, so she probably hasn't come yet.

"......"

It would probably be best to leave now without saying anything. I don't know what Miss Fran was going to give me, but guessing from what she said yesterday, she was probably planning to give me flowers. But even if I take them, they'll just be a burden.

They'll rot eventually, and then I'll have to get rid of them, so there's no point in taking them in the first place. Plus, if I ever see that kind of flower somewhere else again, it'll probably make me think about Miss Fran and this place.

And that's not good for a traveler. It would just make me sad.

"......"

If I leave now, I should be able to finish here without taking any painful memories. So I'd really better get going—

"......Huh?" I suddenly halted.

Flower petals were dancing down from the sky. Red, blue, yellow, pink, purple, and every color you could imagine, fluttering like snowflakes. A sweet scent wafted on the breeze as they drifted down.

Everyone knows something like this doesn't happen naturally. And when I looked up, there she was.

"You got here very early, Elaina. We almost didn't finish our preparations in time."

"Our."

Miss Fran was waving at me, and her students were flying around her, dropping flower petals from the baskets they held in their hands. Every single one of them was smiling.

"Elaina," Miss Fran said from atop her broom, "you chose the life of a traveler for yourself, and so I have no right to hold you back. This is about all I can do."

"Miss Fran…"

"Did it make you happy?"

I answered, sucking in a breath decisively, "Yes, very much so."

I started walking and stepped through the flower-petal rainbow swirling around me.

"Elaina," Miss Fran called out to me again. "As you travel, my students and I will be cheering you on with all our hearts. Never forget that."

I looked up into the sky and replied, "I'll never forget you!"

Finally, I was standing right in front of the gate.

After bowing, the guard made way.

The gently sloping plains stretched out into the distance beyond the wall.

"Elaina." Miss Fran spoke from the air one final time. "Let's meet again someday. Until then, safe travels." Of course, as always, she was smiling.

So I smiled back.

"…Okay!"

○

A broom sped over the plains.

Flowers shimmered in the brilliant sunlight, swaying in the breeze beneath an endless clear blue sky.

Riding on the broom was a witch—a traveler. She was still quite young—in her late teens, to be precise. Her ashen hair billowed behind her, and her lapis lazuli eyes were focused on the horizon dividing the vast plain and the great blue sky. Wearing a black pointy hat and black robe, as well as a star-shaped brooch, she flew on, scattering flower petals in her wake.

She turned her broom toward parts of the world she had not yet seen. What kind of country would she visit next? What kind of people would she meet next? Perhaps a country full of mages, or a country with unreasonably high prices, or maybe the country itself would be in ruins.

Pondering such things, the traveler flew on.

That traveler…who in the world could she be?

That's right. She's me.

Afterword

Nice to meet you; my name is Jougi Shiraishi. This book, *Wandering Witch: The Journey of Elaina*, was self-published on the Amazon Kindle store at the end of 2014, back when I was a total amateur.

My story went through widespread amendments and revisions at the hands of the editing section of GA Books. They were kind enough to point out every single mistake, from mistakes I hadn't noticed on my own to typos and omitted characters that sneaked into the manuscript when it was uploaded to the Kindle store. There are so many odd bits when I go back and read the original...

Anyway, among the reactions from those individuals kind enough to read my book in this era of self-publishing, the most common has been "I can't read the title." My apologies. The characters in the second part of the title are read *journey*. At first I thought, *Since it's about a witch who is traveling, why not simply call it* The Witch's Travels? *That sounds good—let's do that.* But that was a little too simple, and I realized such a title would almost certainly get confused with other titles when people were searching, so I made up a word by doubling the kanji character. It just means *journey*; there's no deeper meaning.

My pen name when self-publishing was Jougi, but as I'm sure you will understand, I didn't appear in any search results. That's why I added my family name to my pen name.

And so I must thank you for picking up a copy of *Wandering Witch: The Journey of Elaina*.

This book is composed of strange stories in which even stranger characters appear. In a nutshell, it's a strange book full of strange tales.

However, nothing makes me happier than the fact that you have added such a book to your collection. By the way, this is just between you and me, but this book is perfect for a bookshelf (although your mileage may vary).

If a second volume of this story comes out, and you line it up next to this volume, I figure that would be even better (again, your mileage may vary).

Well then, on to the thank-yous.

To my manager, M, thank you for all that you do. I'm sure I will continue to cause you headaches as always, but I would be truly happy if you stuck by my side for years to come...

To everyone at SB Creative who decided to start the GA Books editing section, you have my limitless gratitude for picking up my book. Moreover, never in my wildest dreams did I imagine my stories would be included in the launch lineup for a new label. I digress, but when I saw that lineup, I had a moment of panic, like, "Huh? Is it really all right for me to be here among such amazing writers...?" Actually, I still feel that way.

And to Azure, who was in charge of illustrations, thank you for drawing such adorable pictures. Ahhh...Elaina is so cute... Oh no, all the characters are cute... I'm grinning every day looking back at the insert and illustrations, which are just too adorable. Thank you so much.

Finally, to everyone who picked up this book, I'm glad I could make your acquaintance here on these pages. Let's meet again sometime, somewhere. Until next time!